THEY

MARSHALL MILLER

BLUE FORGE PRESS
Port Orchard, Washington

They
Copyright 2023
by Marshall Miller

First eBook Edition July 2023
First Print Edition July 2023

Interior and cover design by Brianne DiMarco

ISBN 978-1-59092-895-0

For information about film, reprint or other subsidiary rights, contact: blueforgegroup@gmail.com

Blue Forge Press is the print division of the volunteer-run, federal 501(c)3 nonprofit company, Blue Legacy, founded in 1989 and dedicated to bringing light to the shadows and voice to the silence. We strive to empower storytellers across all walks of life with our four divisions: Blue Forge Press, Blue Forge Films, Blue Forge Gaming, and Blue Forge Records. Find out more at www. MyBlueLegacy.org

Blue Forge Press
7419 Ebbert Drive Southeast
Port Orchard, Washington 98367
blueforgepress@gmail.com
360-550-2071 ph.txt

MORE BY THE AUTHOR

SPECIAL AGENT KIM KUPAR

Book 1: Jade Eyes
Book 2: They

THE TSCHAAA INFESTATION

Book 1: The Gathering Storm
Book 2: The Tsunami
Book 3: Typhoon of Steel
Free Range Protocol: Tales of the Tschaaa
Beyond the Great Compromise: Tales of the Tschaaa
Survivors: Escaping the Tschaaa

ANTHOLOGIES

Unnerving: Monstrosity
Unnerving: Descent
Unnerving: Wicked
The Mighty Pen
Unconditional
Cascadia
Tales of the Slug
Super: Unexpected Heroes Arise
Naughty & Nice: Stories for Your Stockings

BLUE FLASH

It Begins (The Why Files)
Dragons and Drugs (The Why Files)
Predators and the Press (The Why Files)
Felines and Marriage (The Why Files)
Love is Blue (The Why Files)
The Gentleman and the Tiger (The Why Files)
The Island (The Haunting of Orchard House)
Shane (Angels of Anarchy)

COLLECTED WORKS

Inhumanity: A Year of Stories

This book is dedicated to all the Special Agents and Law Enforcement Personnel I worked with over some thirty years in my career of Protect and Serve. This is especially true with the last group of new and upcoming young agents and other "cops" I worked within my ultimate duty office in Seattle, Washington. You all demonstrated a new level of motivation and professionalism needed in today's trying times.

This story is also dedicated to all the victims of human trafficking, sexual abuse, and child abuse. The organizations mentioned like Polaris are real and deserve our support.

In addition, it is dedicated to our furry family and friends. They often show us how to be better people.

ACKNOWLEDGEMENTS

Of course, this novel would not be possible without the support of my family and friends, especially the furry ones. They were understanding with my late-night writing forays and provided me with the occasional slurpy kiss to remind me I was loved and appreciated. I love you all.

Without the continued support of my current publisher, Blue Forge Press, and the DiMarco Clan, *They* would have been relegated to some old computer file. Thanks again for your tireless support to an old dinosaur.

I hope all the readers enjoy this novel based on my actual experiences.

THEY

MARSHALL MILLER

1.

ally!" Red yelled at her five-year-old daughter as the girl tried to stand hands-free on the top rung of what passed as a playground jungle gym in the 21st Century. The bronze-haired young girl—she took after her mother—looked sheepishly across the daycare playground at her mother.

"Get down from there. Your father and I don't have money for a broken arm or leg."

"And people tell you boys are more risk-takers," said her African-American friend Ebony with a chuckle.

Red and Ebony were nicknames the two mothers embraced. Red (Bridget Morgan), and Ebony (Aliyah Bester), had hit it off from the first day they met at the daycare playground in downtown Seattle. Ebony was trying to chase off a very intoxicated homeless man who

12   THEY

became aggressive toward the children and parents. None of the other mothers (and a couple of fathers) wanted to become involved with a Black woman arguing with some drunk man. Then Bridget stepped up.

"Unless you want to be singing soprano, buddy, time to leave."

Apparently, the drunk saw something in the eyes of the redhead that she meant what she said. The man staggered off, talking to himself.

"Thanks, Red."

"Don't mention it, Ebony."

Both women looked at each other, then burst out laughing. The stereotypical nicknames had just popped out.

Even though they visited each other's homes at least once a week, they called each other by the nicknames they had used that very first day. Their husbands thought they were both a bit nuts.

The two, taller than most women, had become the unofficial leaders at the daycare playground. Their size helped, but their strong wills were evident to all who used the daycare. Ebony and Red soon had all the parents and children organized, welcomed newcomers, and instituted a safety protocol. The two women gave each parent who brought kids to the daycare a whistle to let everyone know someone needed help. Once a month, Red and Ebony ran a "child missing" drill where the sound of a whistle meant all parents grabbed kids and met by the jungle gym/monkey bars. So far, no children had gone missing for more than a few minutes. Everyone watched out for everyone else.

The two women also reached out to Seattle Police Department, developing a respectful working relationship.

"Not all us black people dislike cops," Ebony said.

"Many a redheaded Scot and Irish in my family tree was a cop," added Red.

SPD soon knew that if one of the Terrible Twosome called for help, it was no B.S. call. Thus, the two guardians of the daycare' ensured peace and safety on the playground.

"Any newbies today?" asked Red as she watched her daughter climb down a bit on the jungle gym.

"Yes. A Mrs. Jaswal... Birgitta? I hope I did not mutilate her East Indian name. She has a young daughter, four years of age. Let's see—the name of the girl is Grette."

Red scanned the group of mothers and children. There were no fathers or other males this afternoon.

"Is that her over there, with the lovely Eastern-looking dress?"

"Yes, Red." Ebony frowned as she answered. "She looks like she is trying to find her daughter."

The two women walked quickly over to a frantic-acting woman. Mrs. Jaswal was looking about and talking to herself in her native language with a look of fear only a mother would understand. Her head and body jerked about, and she almost stepped into Red.

"Excuse me, Ma'am. Mrs. Jaswal. Are you looking for Grette?"

Birgitta Jaswal rattled off an answer in her native Punjabi as she waved her hands excitedly. Then she burst into tears and said in English, "She gone! Grette is gone!"

Red blew the All Hands On Deck whistle. Within seconds, mothers grabbed the children and surrounded the jungle gym.

"Okay. We have a four-year-old missing," Ebony's voice boomed out. She held up the mother's cell phone.

"Step up and look at this photo. Then, we run a pattern search as we practiced. Got it? Okay, line up for assignments."

"I just finished a call to SPD, Ebony. They are sending a patrol unit by."

"We'll have the surrounding area searched by the time they arrive. But SPD can at least put out an Amber Alert."

A particular type of Hell descended on the mothers at the daycare. The Hell that it could happen to them.

Kim Kupar stepped off the elevator and into the short hallway, which led to the keycard and combination security door for the Special Agent In Charge, Homeland Security Investigations Office in downtown Seattle,

Washington. Kim tried to suppress a grin, but it felt so *good* to be back at work. Weeks of maternity leave with her newborn fraternal twins was what Kim as a new mother, needed. This was especially true when a nutjob named Roskin came to her home with others to exact some sick revenge, leading to her water breaking as the twins decided it was time. Kim fantasized that her children wanted to pop out and help save Mom. However, her modern Hercules of a husband, Hank, made short work of the intruders.

Kim knew she would be ribbed at the office that Raptor needed help from a non-agent. However, she knew the ribbing would be all in fun.

Hank took paternity leave from the Woodland Park Zoo to help Kim transition back into a work schedule. Eventually, Kim would drop them off at a Federal and State subsidized daycare center within the same square block radius as the HSI office. Hank was having a blast playing a combination of Papa Bear and the senior male lion in a pride, protecting his genetic future. Not for the first time did Kim think how karma had smiled on her when she and Hank reunited. She pushed the thought to the back of her mind about how close she had come to attaching herself to an organized crime figure.

The Special Agent in Charge's administrative assistant, Brenda, met Kim at the entrance door with a smile.

16   THEY

"Welcome back, Kim. Tom Gill wants you to stop and say 'Hi' before you are tied up with anyone else. And you have to share all the new baby pictures with the office to keep us all happy."

Kim tried not to tear up. She had so missed this extended family.

"Of course I will, Brenda. I know my kids will have more honorary Aunts and Uncles than they will know what to do with."

Brenda hugged Kim and then walked her to the SAC's office. Tom Gill met her at his office door.

"Welcome back, Agent Kupar— Kim. This office missed you." As he shook her hand, Kim thought she saw a little twinkle in the eye of the tall, blonde, and imposing senior supervisor.

"Get settled at your desk, and then see ASAC Tim Weiss. I think he may need some of your unique skills."

"Yes, sir. Please thank everyone for all the cards and emails they sent me. I think I have a lot of people volunteering to be aunts and uncles."

"Of course, Kim. LEOs and cops always huddle around children. Contrary to what the media may say, I think it's the 'protect and serve' mentality most of us have."

Kim made a graceful exit and went to her desk. Agents and staff called greetings as she walked through the office. Someone had kept it dusted and cleared off. Kim noticed a card on the government computer keyboard while setting down her handbag. She thought she recognized how her name was scrawled on the envelope as she opened it. It was from Richard Johnson.

"Welcome back, Partner. They made me Acting Group Supervisor for the Forensic Group instead of having ASAC Weiss do double duties. I'm tied up right now, so I can't hug you. Just remember me if you need a babysitter."

Kim smiled as she felt a warmth in her heart. She and Richard had been to Hell and Back with some of the so-called Why Files. Kim sighed. She loved the odd investigations, but now with two children, she sometimes wished to have a chance to investigate more staid subjects. How about an old fashion counterfeit Nike Fraud Investigation?

As she started to sit down, Assistant Special Agent in Charge Tim Weiss stuck his head into her cubicle.

"Oh, sir. I was just about—"

"No need to explain, Kim. Welcome back. I hoped to have time to chew the fat with you," said the brown-haired, mustached, and physically fit supervisor. "Instead, I need your language and culture expertise,"

Kim smiled and felt a little rush of adrenaline; how she had missed challenging work.

After Kim shared pictures of the twins (Rex, the boy named after a particular Agent who came to Kim's rescue, and Guadalupe, after Kim's mother for the girl),

18   THEY

Tim got down to proverbial brass tacks.

"The FBI, for the first time since I can't remember when sent a formal request for HSI assistance. They must have noticed your name and language abilities in the newspapers or court documents as they asked for you. Here, take a look at this request."

Kim scanned the memorandum and frowned.

"A serial kidnapper? One who seems to target children who are primarily People of Color."

"Might be a human trafficker or part of a pedophile ring." Tim Weiss paused, then continued. "Worst case scenario, a serial killer, although no bodies have been found."

"Well, Sir, why specifically ask for me? They must have language specialists."

Tim paused once again. Kim gave him a quizzical look and was about to speak when the ASAC said," The last victim was Punjab. The husband works for your father's company."

"I want my Mommy!"

Grette screamed and cried in Punjabi and English in the dimly lit room. Her screaming was grating on the nerves and eardrums of They. They did not want to apply another dose of ether-soaked cloth due to fears of adverse medical effects on the four-year-old. However, the screams were highly irritating. The cries were also a waste of time in the soundproofed room.

They walked in, and Grette stopped screaming when she saw the cute and colorful teddy bear mask.

"Hello, Grette. I'm Baby Bear. May I talk with you for a moment?"

Grette sobbed and said, "I want my Mommy. I want to go home."

"Well, you can't go home right now. It's not safe. I will tell your Mommy you are safe and sound."

"Why? Why is it not safe?" the dark-skinned little girl asked.

"Oh. It isn't very easy. It is a grownup thing. You know, a grownup like your Mommy and Daddy."

They stepped forward and produced a large sucker from some hidden pocket.

"Here. Lick this until lunch is ready for you and the other children."

"Others?"

"Why, of course, there are other children. All little kids need friends. They are kept safe—like you."

"I can see Mommy later?" Grette asked as she took the sucker.

"Why yes, Grette. You and the others will see your mommies and daddies when safer. Your family will be told you are safe, just like they want."

"Mommy wants me to be safe?"

"Of course she does. Your Mommy loves you. Just like Baby Bear does."

Grette sniffed and began to lick the sucker.

20 THEY

"Here. Take Baby Bear's hand. We will introduce you to some of the other saved children."

They felt a loving warmth when Grette came along quietly. They were doing such good things keeping all the children safe.

God was indeed on their side.

2.

Kim walked up the inclined sidewalk towards the Seattle FBI office. Only some two blocks in downtown Seattle separated HSI and the FBI offices. Of course, the blocks were sloped thanks to Seattle being built on hills surrounding Puget Sound. Downtown Seattle was only a bike rider's paradise when riding downslope. Yet, bike messengers still did bang-up business on their multi-geared bikes.

The strain of walking up the steep grade of Spring Street felt good to Kim. She had been working hard to regain her former shape after giving birth, and it seemed to be paying off. In her attaché case was a letter of introduction. Kim smiled at the formal actions ASAC Weiss took to ensure the FeeBees knew that HSI was doing them a solid favor in allowing a Special Agent just off maternity leave to work with them. Kim knew the political reasons and still thought it was just a lot of penis-waving. She did not care, as completing the mission was a critical matter. Returning kidnapped little children was most important, not who received credit.

At the right time, Kim approached the main entrance to the FBI office building to see hired security officers chasing off some homeless people. Kim found it disheartening that the problems of homeless individuals taking over the sidewalks to an even greater extent than before she took parental/maternity leave. She could tell the three individuals the security officers were rousting were all under the influence of intoxicants. As they walked, shuffled, and staggered down the block, a stream of obscenities emanated from the departing persons.

Kim approached the security displaying her credentials.

"I have an appointment with Agent Audenzia DiStefano."

The female officer smiled as she spoke. "You must mean Audrey DiStefano. She's up on the fifth floor. Come on in the building, and we'll sign you in."

Five minutes later, Kim stepped off the elevator to see a relatively short, dark-haired woman about Kim's age meeting her.

"Agent Kupar? I'm Audrey DiStefano. Pleased to meet you."

"Please call me Kim," the HSI Agent replied as she shook hands. Audrey had a firm handshake, and Kim saw a muscular yet feminine build under Audrey's dark blue business suit. The FBI Agent may be short, but she exuded someone many inches taller, a confident and powerful presence.

"Please follow me and keep your visitor's badge displayed, Kim," advised the FBI Special Agent. "We have some Kens and Karens who love to bitch at people over nothing."

"It is the same all over," replied Kim with a smile.

Audrey led Kim to a small conference room where some case files and photographs were laid out. "Coffee, Kim?"

"I just had some tea, thank you."

Audrey pointed down the adjoining hallway. "Ladies' room down the hall, but I get the vibes you are raring to go."

"Yes, Ma'am. I just returned from parental leave, so missing children are a bit personal to me."

"Huh. As Kipling said, you're a better woman than I am, Gunga Din. If I ever start a family, I don't see me wanting to get back to work any sooner than required."

"I have a fantastic husband who loves to spend time with the twins," Kim said.

"That helps."

Audrey pulled a file from a stack and handed it to Kim.

24 THEY

"Latest victim, number thirteen, a Baker's Dozen. Punjabi, which I understand you speak as a native language."

Kim looked at a photo of the mother and the missing child taken just days before the kidnapping.

"Yes, I do. And as full transparency, the husband works for my family import and export business."

"Well, that fact did not bother my bosses, so it sure does not bother me. It also gives us a personal connection that may help us ascertain if this latest snatch of a child of color relates to the Rainbow Investigation."

"How was that name chosen, Audrey?"

"The children's skin seems to include all the colors of the rainbow. That is the confusing factor. Serial killers' and rapists' profiles often include targeted characteristics of their victims, preferred hair color or age; maybe a subculture like being a sex worker."

"You used the term killers. Any bodies discovered yet?"

"No, Kim. A fact that gives us both hope as well as despair."

Kim gave Audrey a quizzical look. "Why is that?"

"If all the victims are still alive, what horrors are they being exposed to in captivity? The thought of a serial pedophile sharing victims with others—" Audrey's face flushed in anger. Kim paused and looked at her new investigative partner.

"Someone with a passion for solving the problem,

helping the weak," thought Kim. *"Just like me."*

"Audrey, let me review these files to get a good handle on the victims. Then we can hit the ground running. "

"Deal, Kim." Audrey stuck her hand out for a shake. "Put her there, Partner, as they say in Southwest."

Kim chuckled.

"My training officer used to say that and something else."

"What was that, Kim."

"Let's nail the bastards."

Kim was a fast study, so they drove to the Jaswal family home two hours later. During the two hours in the office, Kim soon believed she had found a kindred spirit in law enforcement. They took Kim's car as HSI assigned a take-home vehicle to their agents on call twenty-four/seven. The FBI still tended to make agents sign cars out from a central motor pool.

"You like this Mustang?" asked Audrey.

"It's getting long in the tooth but still runs well. Rumors are that the current administration in D.C. will start buying electric cars for our use."

Audrey snorted derisively. "That'll do just great. There are limited charging stations, and most don't have the get-up and go of these V-6s and V-8s. After a stint in Marine Corps CID, I spent some time in the Border Patrol before the FBI offered me a job. I learned to appreciate some horsepower in a car.”

"You went into the military after high school?”

"Yep. I wanted some action, so I joined the Corps. I wound up in Military Police and spent some time in The Sandbox, Iraq, and Afghanistan. I used the new version of the G.I. Bill and did college. Then I applied for the Marine Corps Criminal Investigation Division. Afterward, I got out, went to the Border Patrol, and applied for the FBI.”

"No Naval Investigative Service?”

Audrey's mouth formed a crooked smile. "I wanted to get away from the military. I thought I'd like being a 'suit.' So I went to Quantico.”

Kim glanced at Audrey, then put her eyes back on the highway. "Well, do you enjoy being a 'suit' in the FBI?”

Audrey laughed. "It has its moments. However, the B.S. paperwork gets old real quick.”

Kim smiled and added, "More than one training officer told me that criminal investigations are like taking a crap. You're not finished until all the paperwork is done.”

Audrey laughed. "You sure you never served in the military? You have a sense of humor like a Jarhead.”

"No, Ma'am. My father had me working in the family business; then, I went into the biological fields and zoology. My father and mother didn't complain much; they thought I'd meet some nice guy through my studies, get married, have kids, and help with the family business."

"Instead, you became a cop."

"Yes. Now I'm married and a new mother. But I can't get the law enforcement bug out of me."

Audrey paused for a minute, then asked. "Mind if I ask you a personal question?"

"Go ahead. I think we'll be working long and hard on this investigation, so no secrets."

"I heard you are the Tiger Lady, as well as Raptor. What gives with the nicknames?"

"Word gets around, doesn't it?"

"Hell, Kim. Law enforcement is based on gossip."

"Well, the quick and dirty story, as T-Rex Moyer would say, is I killed a tiger in India and kicked ass in and out of the office. Thus, Raptor was a handle I was given, but circumstances led to my involvement with more felines."

"The Why Files?"

Kim laughed.

"I knew the FBI would hear about those cases. After all, Mulder and Scully made you all famous."

Audrey chuckled. "The ghost of J.Edger Hoover refuses to let any other agency grab the limelight."

"Well, some of the cases are still classified. However, the fact that Chinese organized crime created a saber-tooth cat a long time ago hit the news. So, I'm back to being a Tiger Lady."

28 THEY

"Well, Kim, it could be worse."

"How so, my new friend?"

"You could be considered a Cougar on the prowl, which may piss off your husband."

The two women laughed at the image of an aging female agent hanging out in bars picking up sexual partners.

"*I think Audrey could become a dear friend,*" Kim thought. A close female law enforcement type would be good. Sometimes, a woman needed to bounce ideas off of another woman.

The pair of investigators were soon at the West Seattle address. The Jaswal family had purchased an older house built near World War II and then modernized it. Whoever had performed the rebuild had kept the original designs and structure. Kim bet herself that the original hardwood floors would remain almost entirely intact.

"If this is a traditional Punjabi home, the husband is definitely the man of the house. They are Hindu, not Sikh like my father. Sometimes that can be a bone of contention."

Audrey smiled.

"Well, I was raised Roman Catholic. Now I practice being a good person and go to Mass at Christmas. How about you?"

Kim shrugged. "I grew up with Sikh gurus and Argentine Catholic priests. I was married in a Catholic

Church and had Sikh celebrations afterward. So I guess my belief system is rather convoluted."

Audrey nodded and pulled out her credentials case.

"Please let me introduce us in Hindi or Punjabi, Audrey, whatever seems comfortable."

The FBI Agent smiled. "Whatever greases us in and starts a conversation is fine with me."

Kim rang the doorbell and looked at the well-kept, old-fashioned wood porch. The Agents heard a male voice speak as footsteps approached the door, then a sizeable dark-skinned man opened the door. The husband and father examined the two women with stern gazes.

"Namaste," Kim said as she placed her hands together, palms touching, and bowed.

The man returned the gesture as he said in the King's English, "May I help you?"

"I am Special Agent Kim Kupar, and this is FBI Special Agent Audrey DiStefano. We have been assigned to help recover your daughter, Grette."

The man smiled. "You are my employer's well-known daughter. Your father, Balraj Singh, often brags about you in the office."

Kim tried not to blush as Audrey chuckled.

"Birgitta!" the man called out. "We have guests. Some tea, please."

"Please come into our home, ladies. I am Balvir,

30 THEY

Grette's father."

Kim moved to remove her shoes, and Balvir motioned to stop. "No need for that, Kim Kupar. My wife and I have adopted some actions which are customary in America. We are Christian converts, which still seems a rarity to some, at least to people from the Punjab region."

Balvir led the two agents into a well-kept living room and motioned for them to sit on an overstuffed sofa. Kim noticed a child peeking around a room entry corner. Balvir saw the 'spy' and said, *"Come here"* in Punjabi. The young boy immediately went to his father's side and stood partially behind Balvir.

"Come, Bahadur. Please do not be rude to our guests. Greet them as I taught you."

The young man stepped forward. "Namaste," Bahadur said as he bowed slightly with prayerful hands. "Pleased to meet you," the young man added.

Audrey copied Kim and greeted him with "Namaste," adding, "Please to meet you, young man."

"Kim is my employer's daughter, you heard about in school," said his father. "Miss DiStefano is an FBI Agent."

The smaller version of Balvir's eyes widened a bit. "Are you a Tiger Lady too?" he asked.

"Nah," Audrey replied with a smile. "I'm more of a dog person."

Kim said, trying not to blush, "I guess my story has

gotten around."

"Your story, as you say, is well known among the East Indian community, even without your father's comments," replied Balvir. "It is not often that our community has a local heroine."

Kim smiled. "I just do my job, Mr. Jaswal. This is why Agent DiStefano and I are here. We want to discuss your missing daughter with you and your wife."

Birgitta arrived with the tea, taking a few moments to serve the Agents. After the obligatory sip, Kim began the conversation.

"I know you went over the situation with the local police, Mrs. Jaswal. However, Agent DiStefano and I would like to review the events and see if you remember any other details."

"What is there to add?" asked the wife and mother sitting next to her husband. "One minute, she was playing with the other children. The next—" Birgitta's chin began o quiver as she blinked back tears.

"Do you know who would want to take your child?" asked Audrey. "Is there anyone who communicated a threat because of a personal conflict? Anyone with a grudge?"

"No," replied the father and husband. "We have not even run into the racial strife many say exists in this area. All of our neighbors have been welcoming and supportive."

"A mother of one of the children at the daycare

center started a GoFundMe page on the internet," said Birgitta. "She wants to keep organizing searches for Grette—" her voice cracked, and she sobbed. Balvir hugged with a strong arm and whispered words of comfort.

"We are here to do what we can to find your missing daughter," interjected Kim. "The FBI and Homeland Security placed this investigation at the top of importance."

"I wish we could tell you more, Agents," said Balvir. "However, we are baffled why our daughter was chosen—to take."

"Please call us anytime, day or night, Mister Jaswal," added Audrey. "We special agents are on call twenty-four seven. That's why we are paid."

The parents stood, signaling to Kim and Audrey it was time to leave. The two investigators gave the grieving couple their business cards and reiterated they could be called anytime, day or night.

"Even with you having two young children?" said Balvir to Kim with a smile.

"I see my father prevents me from having any secrets."

"Every father welcomes grandchildren into the family."

"Well, sir, I have a very understanding and supportive husband. Hank is more than willing to take care of twins."

"Supportive and loving husbands help us get thru the difficult times," said Brigette as she smiled at her husband. He placed a protective arm around his love.

"We men do what we can, what we must."

Just then, young Bahadur stepped forward with something in his hand.

"I would like you to have this, Tiger Lady," the young man said as he handed Kim a figure riding an animal.

"What's that, Kim?" asked Audrey.

"Hindu Goddess Durga, the protective goddess of the universe."

"Is that a tiger she is riding?"

Balvir smiled. "We may be Christian, but certain older beliefs are hard to disregard." He grinned at his son, adding, "Especially for the young."

Kim smiled at Bahadur. "Thank you, Bahadur. I am sure Durga's spirit will help us in the investigation.

"Bring my sister home. Please. I miss her."

Audrey noticed a look of pride in the boy's father's eyes as she spoke. "We'll do our best, Bahadur. I promise."

The two federal agents took their leave and went back to their vehicle. Kim drove the Mustang out of the West Seattle neighborhood and asked Audrey, "Any ideas on the next step?"

"First, we stop someplace for a sit down with some coffee. Then we decide who we talk with next."

34 THEY

"Sounds good to me, although I'll order some tea. Any location suggestions?"

"Local, not a chain if possible. I like to support Mom and Pop operations, Kim."

"Okay. We'll find one."

A quarter of an hour later, the two special agents sat in a local West Seattle coffee shop. They found a private table towards the back of the shop.

After sipping her coffee, Audrey said, " I think we need to talk with your father to see if he or the company has received any threats."

Kim sighed, then answered, "I agree. I want to think my father would call me if anyone threatened him or his company. However, he is stubborn and prideful at times. The thought of asking his daughter for help—well, I think the expression is it would stick in his craw."

"Male and fatherly egos often get in the way," said Audrey. "After becoming a Marine, my father still talked down to me." She paused. "However, there was another elephant between him and me in the room."

"If I can be nosey and ask you about the elephant?" asked Kim.

"Might as well. I see this as being a long-involved investigation," Audrey replied. She paused for a moment, then spoke. "I'm gay—a lesbian. I don't have a partner yet. Hopefully, that does not offend any of your sensibilities."

Kim grinned. "Ever read the Kama Sutra? That

Indian literary work was about sex, including graphic descriptions of homosexual relations between servants and masters."

"But your mother is Roman Catholic."

"Thus, Audrey, I don't discuss certain subjects in detail with my mother. She is now as happy as a clam that I'm married with children. If I quit my job, she would be in heaven."

Kim did not mention her sexual liaison with a certain Chinese Triad member. She wondered how much of that story had reached the FBI.

"Well, Kim, my sexual identity has raised some eyebrows in the FBI. J. Edger may have been homosexual, but he sure as Hell did not like his Agents being anything but straight. That attitude still hangs on in some offices."

Kim sipped her Earl Grey tea and replied, "We women enter a male-dominated career field when we became criminal investigators. Old stereotypes die hard. A female instructor at our academy warned us about how we would be stereotyped based on our dress."

Audrey chuckled. "Let me guess, Kim. The ole Dyke Versus Slut comments."

"You heard it also."

"And once my sexual orientation became known, many whispers involving the 'D-word' floated around. When I let it be known that as a Former Marine, I was more than willing to brace anyone who talked about me behind my back, the comments seem to dry up." Audrey sipped her coffee and then continued. "But there still seems to be hesitancy about how to talk to me. Am I one of the guys who want to hear dirty jokes, or am I a Me-Too movement-type looking to yell at someone?"

Kim paused in thought before replying. "I had to deal with the male tendency not to believe a woman could be tough. I was tested on more than one occasion."

Audrey grinned as she answered. "We heard about some of your ass-kicking in our office. I think the question of 'tough' was answered."

Kim smiled. Audrey had a refreshing honesty. "Well, Audrey, I have had to lay hands on some members of the male gender in the last few years, as well as one female miscreant."

"I understand you are well-trained in East Indian martial arts, Kim."

"*Kalaripayattu.* Some say it and other forms are the basis for all Asian Martial Arts."

"I got into Shorin-Ryu Karate in high school," replied Audrey. "I decided I needed to deal with any bullying when I eventually came out as a lesbian."

"Maybe we could work out together sometime, compare styles," added Kim.

"Any time. The guys in the office seem to be afraid a gal will show them up."

The two agents finished their beverages and hit

the proverbial road. The trip to the offices of *Kupar Electronics/Computer Imports and Exports* was quick and uneventful. The combination office complex and warehouse was located a few blocks East of the major Port of Seattle piers. Kim's father, Balraj Singh Kupar, had spent reasonable sums rebuilding the post-World War II building. Thus, it was clean and neat, with painted Asian designs along the outer walls and entranceway. Balraj had hired his security force to keep any homeless encampment from being established and keep the area in excellent condition. Kim also knew her father had an 'agreement' with Seattle Police Department that there would be no complaints if they came and helped him enforce no trespassing notices. Whether correct or not, SPD looked the other way if the security force thumped some street drug addicts.

"I think your family has money," said Audrey as she scanned the area. "So, I will have to say if I were you, I would have stayed in the family business."

"Even if you were bored to tears at times?" replied Kim.

Audrey grinned as she replied, "I get your point. I would still have joined the Marines if it were my family."

The security officers smiled at Kim as they let her park in the management parking lot. She came around often enough for them to recognize the boss's daughter. Kim did not know that her father made all the employees memorize family photos. Woe is the person who disrespected his family. East Indian sensibilities concerning castes died hard.

A young, nervous security officer escorted the two Agents to the private elevator to Balraj's office on the business's top floor. Balraj Singh Kupar met them at his office suite door.

"So my daughter deigns to visit her father on her first day back to work," Balraj said, grinning. "And she brings a friend. The stars must be in alignment."

He looked at Andrey and said," Excuse me while I give Kim an unprofessional fatherly hug."

Audrey grinned back as she replied, "But of course, Sir."

Balraj Kupar wore a dark Brooks Brothers suit rather than some traditional East Indian garb. He also no longer wore his hair long and wrapped in a turban in the conventional Sikh manner. Balraj was a successful Western Style businessman and wished to be perceived as such. However, he kept many of the other tenants of the Gurus. His daughter tended to melt his often staid demeanor.

Kim hugged her father and smiled. Since the Jade Palace shootout, she and her father seemed much closer. Of course, Kim's mother, Guadalupe, had scolded him for not paying more attention to Kim since she left the family business, which seemed to aid in the matter.

And now Kim had given him grandchildren, the icing on the cake.

"So, to what do I owe this auspicious visit?" Balraj said after leaving the embrace.

"First, Father, let me introduce Special Agent Audrey Distefano of the Federal Bureau of Investigation."

Balraj offered a hand to shake, which prevented Audrey from deciding to "Namaste" or go for a traditional business greeting.

"The FBI! This meeting must be of some import, not just for pleasure."

"Unfortunately, Mister Kupar, it is far from a social meeting."

A young lady appeared pushing a wheeled service with coffee and tea. Neither Kim nor Audrey declined the offer despite just having finished like beverages. The social drinking of coffee and tea helped them to relax, which could be a stressful interview.

Audrey sipped her demitasse coffee and grinned. "Sir, I could have used this coffee many nights in the Marine Corps. It packs a jolt."

"Strong tea and coffee served Kim's uncle and me well during our time in the Indian Army." Balraj sipped at his coffee as Kim sipped her tea. "Some of my employees talk about 'cowboy coffee' here in America. Beans or grounds are thrown in a pan and boiled over a campfire. I imagine most military-style coffee resembles that worldwide." The father looked at his daughter with a twinkle in his eye.

"I steered my daughter Kim away from the military and into more intellectual pursuits. Then she becomes a special agent, is involved in gun battles, and gives her mother gray hairs."

"Now, Father—"

"I joke, my daughter. You have brought honor to our family. Never forget that."

Audrey felt jealous as she saw the interplay between father and daughter. She shoved such thoughts to the back of her mind; this investigation was too essential to let personal feelings intrude.

"Well, Father, unfortunately, the purpose of this meeting is not a happy one."

"This is about a certain missing child, yes?" asked Balraj.

"Yes. We have to ask some hard questions."

"Ask away, Kim, Agent DiStefano. I look at my business as a family. Once someone attacks a family member, we band together to help."

"So, Sir," said Audrey, "have you had any threats from strangers? Or maybe a disgruntled employee out for revenge over some perceived slight?"

"No, Agent. We try to part ways with former employees amicably. Even those I have fired, I give a small severance package. The Chinese Triad did not even come after the company due to Kim's involvement in the Jade Palace shootout and arrests. "

"Do you know if Mister Jaswal made any serious

enemies at work? Have you heard of anyone wanting to harm him or his family?"

"No, Ma'am. Any disagreements in the workplace have been minor. "

"Father, would you let us look at your security tapes?" interjected Kim. "We would be looking for visitors, delivery drivers, and those who may not be who they claimed to be."

"Of course. Anything I can do to help recover little Grette. Anyone who seizes a little girl like that—if only Shiva were real and could manifest as the Destroyer."

"We'll return when you can collect the videos."

"So it takes an investigation for the daughter to visit the father?" Balraj said with a grin.

"Father, you know I will visit with the twins as soon as possible."

"I know, Kim. It is just the father in me to push my little girl even though she is now a grown and successful woman."

Balraj escorted the two Agents out and shook Andrey's hand as she departed.

"I can tell you work well with my daughter and hopefully help keep her out of trouble."

"Although I think she handles trouble quite well, I will watch her back, Sir."

"Stop by anytime. A friend of my daughter is a friend of mine."

Audrey spoke as the two investigators left the

parking area in Kim's government vehicle.

"I must admit, Kim, I envy your relationship with your father. He is pretty proud of you."

Kim sighed as she replied, "It was not always so. My father seemed disappointed because I took a non-traditional role as a woman and did not stick with the family business, get married, and have kids."

"Then the whole bit with the Sabre Tooth Cat and company happened," said Audrey.

"I see you and the FBI did some checking on me."

"Hey, I had to know who I was teaming up with on this case," answered Audrey. "What if I got stuck with some prig who took it as a personal affront that I'm Lesbian? I have enough problems dealing with the idea that I was given this case to fail."

Kim glanced at her new 'partner' and then focused on the road.

"You're serious, aren't you?"

"Yep. If I screw up, the Agency has a perfect scapegoat to blame. The kids don't get recovered, but until bodies turn up, management can hem and haw and continue the investigation with some fair-haired boy. If a body does turn up, the FBI suits say they have a new set of eyes dealing with the missing kids while pushing the locals to take some action. After all, the assumption is that kidnapping involves crossing state lines. Unless a body is found outside Washington State, the FBI has some wiggle room for who is ultimately responsible for the outcome."

"My God, Audrey. The idea that the children are just political pawns makes my blood boil."

"Well, reading between the lines of what I know about how your organization treated you, I can safely say Homeland Security has its own political animals in management."

Kim had to mentally agree that HSI had its share of people who cared more about their careers than doing the right thing, even when children were involved.

"So, you still think I am not a prig?" asked Kim.

Audrey laughed,

"Far from it! You act like a hardass member of the Corps. How you juggle twins, a husband willing to stay at home but can still kick ass (I read the police report), and come back to work on a high visibility case is beyond me."

Kim had to laugh. She just did what she believed was suitable for her and her family. She never thought of herself as special other than being a Special Agent.

"I appreciate your honesty, Audrey, but I am far from unique. I was just forced into strange circumstances."

"Yeah, right. And I have a used Puget Sound Viaduct to sell you; it's in pieces now."

"So, my turn, Audrey. Why the envy of my dad and me? Are you estranged, I guess is the word, from your father?"

44   THEY

"Hah! Estranged is a fancy word for no longer talking to each other. The old 'L-word' is not in his vocabulary."

"So he did not accept your sexual identity."

"Hell, he downright threw it at me like a rock." Audrey's face flushed with anger. "That was one reason why I joined the Corps. I wanted a family, a sister, and a brotherhood of people who would accept you as you are as long as you do your job. So in 2012, I joined up."

"How was it? I was never in the military."

"The laws had changed by then, but some of the 'old crew' still had trouble accepting lesbians. We women still had separate basic training units, but as I went into Military Police, I received the same combat training as the rest of the Corps."

Audry chuckled.

"I had to deck another woman when she called me a 'Dyke', not a guy as you would suppose. But like they say, once a Marine, always a Marine, never an Ex-Marine."

"And you saw combat."

"Yep. Sniped at in Iraq as Obama shut us down, then went on convoy operations in Afghanistan. I was not around for the Afghanistan Biden Bug-Out, thank God. Technically, I'm still in the Inactive Reserve."

"My father and Uncle were in the Indian military and talked about it. I never was, so sometimes I wonder if I would have measured up to their standards."

Audrey laughed. "The Tiger Lady wonders if she would measure up. You can neither confirm nor deny, but the Bureau schmoozed enough information that I know you were in the proverbial shit on numerous occasions. I'm a pretty good judge of character. You would have had no problem being a Marine."

Audrey's comments gave Kim a nice warm feeling. Walking around like a beached whale pregnant made many women wonder if their life and body would ever return to a higher standard. Audrey's comments said she would.

"Well, back to the offices to look for updates?"

"Yes, Kim. The Bureau in Seattle hates it when we are gone for very long. Afterward, want to stop for a beer? "

"I would, except I am breastfeeding. Breast milk and beer don't mix well. I use a breast pump at home so my husband Hank doesn't have to use baby formula. That is my stop after work."

Audrey smiled. "You are a better woman than I am, Kim. I think I'd be looking for a wet nurse. Or maybe figure out a way for men to lactate."

Both women laughed at the thought of that image.

Baby Bear watched as the children ate their lunch under the watchful eye of the Minions. Baby Bear and Baby Fox had identical smiles under their masks, clothes, and matching physical builds. Their Minions wore similar jumpsuits and similar top-of-the-line costume character masks. Although top-of-the-line, none of the Minion's masks were as detailed as Baby Bear and Baby Fox. No Minions exuded the aura of authority as Baby Bear and Baby Fox. Every human in the large dining room knew who was in charge.

The thirteen young children—the oldest just turned seven and the youngest was Grette at age four—were happy, giggling, smiling, with some holding hands with their friends. The food was excellent, with childhood favorites of mac and cheese, hotdogs, and Spaghetti-Os. The good food and companionship were combined with an extraordinary mix of medications to keep the thirteen children happy and content while awaiting a 'safe' reuniting with family.

Baby Bear signed as he felt the love and affection of the thirteen children.

"It is satisfying to do God's Work," said Baby Fox.

"Yes, it is. Even without these smiling faces, we know the Lord needs and appreciates this work."

Baby Fox looked at Baby Bear and asked, "Do you think it is time for the World to know God's Will?"

"Soon. Very soon. God will let us know the exact time."

Baby Bear and Baby Fox knew the other was grinning under the mask.

Like a virus, God's Joy was contagious.

It was late when Kim finally arrived home. She entered the front door and yelled, "Honey, I'm home!" Then Kim realized how she sounded like a character in the 1950s and 60s television comedies. Special Agent Knows Best? Leave It To HSI? Kim knew she was tired when her mind began fantasizing.

Hank met her in the living room, a twin in each arm, and kissed Kim quickly. Both Rex and Guadalupe looked tired but would accept Mommy's breast.

"How was your first day back?"

"You will not believe it. Let me give the kids a snack, and I'll tell you the whole story."

After feeding and putting the twins to bed, Kim cuddled with her husband and explained the day's events.

"First day back, you get slammed with a high-profile case," observed Hank.

"That's what I get for fluency in several languages. The FBI was smitten with my 'Tiger Lady' persona. Plus, the last victim's father is an employee of my father. So, a perfect storm."

"Well, that's what you get for doing a good job: more work."

Kim snuggled closer. She was so glad this bear of a man was in her life. "They put me in for early promotion to Senior Special Agent. Office rumors are I am being groomed for a supervisor job."

"Is that good or bad?"

Kim sighed as she answered. "I would have a bunch of people's headaches, not just my own. I love my work, but with the twins—"

"Don't you worry, Kim. This senior pride male will watch over our cubs when you are away. You do what makes you happy. Just stay safe, love."

Kim looked up at Hank, then kissed him.

"I am so lucky to have you, dearest Hank. You are a shining example of a good husband and father. I love you."

"I love you also, Kim. Always remember that."

"I will. Now kiss me again, my large lover."

Kim met Audrey at the FBI office the next day. Over coffee and tea, they mapped out their investigative steps.

"So, Audrey. Do we start looking at serial pedophiles? The one characteristic that links all the victims is that they are young children."

"Yeah, Kim. The sickest of the sick go after minors. How someone finds sexually undeveloped children to be erotic is beyond me. I know Homeland Security does much work with child pornography in their Cyber Unit. Do you have any local connections?"

"Yes, we do. A Special Agent in my office, Ly Trang, has a sister who works with the Washington State Depart of Corrections and handles sex offenders out on community release. She may have heard rumors from the people she supervises and checks on."

"Let's stop by your office and hook up with Agent Trang. He can schmooze us in with his sister."

The two federal agents walked down the hill to the HIS office building. On the 23rd Floor, Kim introduced Audrey to ASAC Weiss.

"Glad we can be of service, Agent DiStefano."

"Yes, Sir. I'm personally glad Agent Kupar is available to assist. This Rainbow Investigation is not an easy case."

"No, it is not. Please tell me if you need anything. This case is on the front burner."

"Sir, we were about to talk to Ly Trang to arrange a meeting with his sister at Community Supervision," said Kim. "We hope one of the previous sex offenders on community release may have heard something."

"Go where the investigation takes you, Kim. You have our support."

They sat down with Ly Trang in an interview room five minutes later. Ly skimmed the file, then punched in his sister's cellphone number. There was a quick conversation in Vietnamese, and then Ly hung up.

"Bao is expecting you," said Ly. "She may call an offender or two into the office to talk."

"Good. Thanks, Ly. I owe you."

"Any time, Kim. It is bad enough to be a young refugee. To be kidnapped when you think you are loved and safe? That is an exceptional horror. "Ly paused, then continued. "Is one of the missing Vietnamese?"

"Yes. A young boy."

"Call me if you need information from the Vietnamese community. All the children are dear to us. There is a special Hell for those who would harm a child."

Betty and Barney's Daycare in Tacoma, Washington, was neither the low-end nor the high-end of the childcare industry. It accurately represented the 'middle,' an average business that provided a service for parents who needed someplace for their children while working. The daycare could house a dozen young children, ages three to eight, on any given day.

On this particular day, young and blonde seven-year-old Wendy Watson was hanging out at the daycare after school. Her mother refused to allow her to be a Latchkey Kid at home, so the school bus dropped Wendy off daily in front of the daycare.

Wendy felt herself a mature and worldly seven-year-old, so she did not deal with most other children. Instead, Wendy watched.

Thus, Wendy watched when five-year-old Jimmy Brown climbed the six-foot chainlink fence to achieve freedom. Jimmy was a biracial child with a Port Wine birthmark covering two-thirds of his face. To say his early life was a challenge was an understatement. Jimmy climbed as Wendy slowly walked toward him.

"Jimmy, why are you leaving?"

"Other kids look at me funny," was the reply.

"So why care? They aren't anything special."

Just then, a person wearing a costume cat mask approached where Jimmy climbed.

"Are you trying to escape to safety?" Cat Mask asked.

Jimmy looked at him in confusion.

"Here, let me help you." Cat Mask reached for Jimmy, straddling the top of the fence.

"We don't talk to strangers or let them touch us," Wendy stated with authority. "Only First Responders can touch us."

Timmy started to squirm in the grasp of the stranger.

"I'd let him go before I start screaming," warned Wendy as she approached the fence.

"Go away, little white girl," Cat Mask said. "This is the will of the Lord."

Wendy had been taught by her mother not to suffer from strangers. Especially strangers were wearing masks and talking weirdly. Wendy was also trained to keep a sharpened Number Two pencil handy and use it. Cat Mask screamed when the little white girl stabbed the pencil into the belly button of the stranger.

Cat Mask lashed out with a vicious kick that slammed the chainlink fence into Wendy's face. The seven-year-old toppled back, and her head hit the packed earth hard. Jimmy pulled back from Cat Mask and fell off this perch and onto Wendy. Cat Mask scrambled down the street as adults responded to the screams.

3.

The Department of Corrections Community Supervision Office, where Bao Trang worked, was near an area of Tacoma ofttimes called the industrial zone. It was considered an older part of the city, not far from warehouses and wholesale establishments. Kim found a visitor's parking spot in the attached fenced-in lot. The Agents checked in at the entry desk, and Bao Trang had one of the office staff escort them back to her office. Kim saw the family resemblance between her and her brother Ly as she entered Bao's office; seated across from the Community Supervision Officer was why Bao did not meet them at the entrance.

A man of European descent sat across from his community supervisor and met the two female Agents with his eyes. Immediately Kim saw the gaze of a human being haunted by their past and possibly the present.

"Agent Kupar," said Bao with a smile as she stood and shook hands with Kim and Audrey. "My brother has sung your praises often."

"Please call me Kim. Audrey DiStefano from the FBI, and I hope you might have some information to help us with this investigation."

Bao looked at the seated man. "James Cannon might have some inside knowledge, right, James?"

"Yes, Ma'am. Maybe."

Bao found a couple of extra chairs and then closed the office door. They sat in silence for a few moments, and then James spoke. "I am a sex offender under Officer Trang's supervision. The Department of Corrections wants us called 'clients' now, but I know what I did. Sugarcoating anything does no one any good."

"Confession is good for the soul?" asked Audrey.

"Yes, it can be if it is a truthful confession, not just bullshit to scam people and the system."

"Mister Cannon is involved in an intensive treatment program as part of his supervised release. Why don't you explain it to the Agents."

James took a deep breath and then spoke. "Once a month, I spend an entire weekend in Doctor Rebecca Murray's psychiatric clinic with other sex offenders. We open up about our thoughts, dreams, and—desires we felt. We are also put on the 'box,' a lie detector, by a highly experienced examiner to ensure no holding back. Everyone there knows about everyone else."

"Sounds like a super A.A. meeting," said Kim.

"I have heard that comment before. The bottom line is it helps us deal with our demons."

"And can you be specific about those demons?" prodded Officer Bao. "These Agents need to know where you come from fundamentally. They have to be sure what you say has a basis in reality."

Kim saw the ghosts appear in Jame's eyes as he spoke.

"For as long as I can remember, my world revolved about sex, orgasms, masturbation. We are talking from before age five. It did not matter the gender or age of the persons involved. If it felt good sexually, I did it." The offender/client paused, then continued. "Then I was finally caught having sex with a twelve-year-old. I was thirty."

"Which gender?" asked Audrey.

"Does it matter? I groomed them, then porked them."

"A relative?"

"A cousin."

"So, what is your goal now, Mister Cannon?" asked Kim.

James Cannon paused for a good minute. Then he answered. "I want to be able to go fishing with my nieces and nephews. I want to be able to interact with people, especially minors. I want to be able to talk to people—"

Kim watched as James gripped the arms on his chair as if to crush them.

"I want the demon thoughts out of my head, my soul."

The three women and one man sat in silence; then Kim spoke. "So. What do you know that may help us in an investigation involving multiple kidnappings of young children?"

"Like I said, everyone has to open up about everything when we have the required weekend retreats. That includes people they have met, people who approached them, and groups they contacted or which contacted them." The offender sipped at his cup of coffee and then continued. "One participant, Walter Jenkins, talked about this group of adults he bumped into wearing costume masks. He was at Metro Parks near South Nineteenth. Walter said they had a couple of little kids with them. He is not supposed to hang around city or county parks where minors are known to be present."

"What made him suspicious? Why did he mention this contact?"

James smirked as he answered. "If he didn't, and the Doctor found out, a quick call to his Corrections Community Supervisory Officer and bang! He is violated and back in prison. If you do something, the doctor finds questionable, that can be viewed as a violation of your conditions of release."

"So he talked with these people?" asked Audrey.

"Hell, the idiot followed them to this old building with them. Walter violated his conditions by closely contacting those kids without approved supervision. He told the group he heard other kids singing until someone shut a door, then it was silence. Walter said it was like a sound studio he worked in before imprisonment. Shut a door, and it's all soundproofed."

"Walter was caught molesting little girls while a sound technician at a local recording studio," interjected Bao.

"What else did he say?" asked Kim.

"He was excited and started babbling about how happy the two kids seemed and how nice the people in the masks were."

"He never thought it was strange, all these adults wearing masks?"

"Hell, after this Corona Virus, nobody questions people masking up. It used to be if you went into a bank with a Halloween mask, the guard would ask you to leave. Now, no one questions any masking up."

"Were the kids wearing masks?"

"Nah. Walter started talking about how cute the little Asian girl was, then spoke about the little black boy. Finally, Doctor Murray shut him down. In front of the group, she said Walter demonstrated a continued unhealthy fixation with little children. The doctor questioned Walter whether he was serious about dealing with what led to his imprisonment."

"Damn!" said Audrey. "No doctor and patient confidentiality?"

"Agent, we sign waivers up the yin-yang to attend these groups and participate in these sharing exercises. There are no secrets. The first thing you learn about sexual abuse is it is based on people keeping secrets. It happens in the shadows. Thus, we have no secrets. We can't hide anything from anybody."

"So, Walter eventually shut up?" asked Kim.

"Yes. But we all knew Walter was in trouble thanks to his babbling."

"Jenkins was told to report to his CSO," interjected Bao. "So far, he is a no-show. By the end of the day, there will be a warrant for his arrest for violating his release conditions."

Kim looked at Audrey. "If Walter can help us find this location—"

"Oh, Kim, he'll help," said Bao. "Otherwise, he'll be in McNeil Island until he rots."

Kim's cell phone chimed. "Excuse me," Kim said and stepped outside the office.

Audrey looked at James. "So, James. What do you think about this situation?"

"I think Walter does not want to be cured. And the people kidnapping kids are just as sick."

"Do you have thoughts about—little children?"

"I try not to, Agent. I pray to God not to have such evil thoughts ever again."

Kim stepped back into the office and spoke. "Time to go. There was an attempt at another daycare center."

"Good Luck," said James Cannon. "You'll need it."

Baby Bear was not happy. Baby Cat lay on a padded medical table, yelped in pain as Baby Rabbit poked and prodded.

"That lead pencil left some pieces behind," said Baby Rabbit.

"It hurts!" complained Baby Cat.

"Why did you try to grab that child?" asked Baby Bear as Baby Fox entered the room carrying something.

"I saw the Lord's Work at hand. The small boy with the birthmark on his face, trying to escape the daycare cent— *ouch!*"

"So God, Our Lord, spoke to you?"

"Well—in a way."

"And what way was that?" asked Baby Fox.

"I just knew the little boy needed to be helped— and saved."

If Baby Bear's forehead could be seen under the mask, people would notice a severe frown.

"So you then grabbed the little boy, the little girl stabbed you with a pencil, and you smashed the girl to the ground."

"Baby Bear, I didn't mean to hurt her!"

"But you did. And this incident is on the radio and television. So everyone knows just how injured the poor little white girl is, thanks to you."

"I'm sorry, Baby Bear, Baby Fox! I am so sorry."

Baby Fox handed Baby Bear the something brought in.

"Yes. You are a very sorry individual,"

The scythe nearly took Baby Cat's head off with one swipe. Baby Bear swore in frustration when it took a second cut.

"Baby Bear!" said Baby Fox. "Language!"

Kim and Audrey badged their way into the crime scene at *Betty and Barney's Day Care.* As the Special Agents approached, Tacoma Detective Stan Fornier was speaking with Barney Stubble, the Barney in the business name. The Detective waved the Agents over.

"I didn't think I'd see Seattle people here."

"Well, Stan, we're handling a related case out of Seattle," Audrey replied. "You know Kim Kupar from Homeland Security?"

The large and wide black detective smiled as he answered. "By reputation only, but please to meet you, Tiger Lady."

"I can see rumors proceed me," said Kim as she shook hands.

"So   what   brings   you   ladies   to   this

attempted molestation?"

"We'd like to question the owner, staff, and children involved."

"This here is Barney Stubble, half-owner of the daycare. He was just telling me about hearing the screams."

A very nervous older, plump, light-complected man wiped his sweaty brow with a faded handkerchief.

"I'm Special Agent Kim Kupar, Homeland Security Investigations, and with me is Special Agent Audrey DiStafeno of the Federal Bureau of Investigations. We want to ask you a few questions about this possible abduction attempt."

"Like I told the Detective, I heard a scream and came running."

"So there was no adult in the playground area."

"Well—"

"I think we have established that Barney and his wife Betty are operating understaffed," interjected Stan.

"Do you have security cameras?" asked Audrey.

"Yes."

"We'll need to see the recordings. And is the little African American boy still here? I know the little girl was taken to the hospital."

"Yes, Jimmy is still here. We are having trouble getting ahold of his parents."

Kim looked at Audrey as she spoke. "Shall we? He's young, but he may have a detail that will help.

Hopefully, his parents won't be too upset about us talking with him before they arrive. However, we need to strike while the proverbial iron is hot."

Detective Fornier saw the logic of letting two women talk to Jimmy as children often trusted women more as part of the 'mother' image. He kept Barney busy collecting the surveillance tapes as Kim and Audrey walked over to a bench in the playground. Betty, the other half of the ownership, tried to keep Jimmy isolated while watching the remaining children at the daycare.

"You more police?" asked the ample light-skinned woman.

"Yes, Ma'am. Special Agents Kupar and DiStefano. We need to ask Jimmy a few questions while the events are fresh in his mind."

"I didn't want to cause any trouble," blurted out Jimmy. "I just wanted to go home."

Kim smiled as she sat down next to Jimmy.

"You're not in trouble with us, Jimmy," she said. "In fact, we need your help."

"You do?"

"Why yes," Audrey answered as she sat on the bench. "Can you tell us what the man who grabbed you when you were on the fence looked like?"

Jimmy's brow was furrowed in thought.

"I think it was a man. It was hard to tell as a mask covered the face. The mask made the voice sound funny."

"What kind of mask, Jimmy?" asked Kim.

"It was a cat mask. I think it was a guy as he grabbed me hard like a man would."

"What kind of clothes was the person wearing?"

"Coveralls, like my dad wears when he works at the garage. But they were clean, not greasy from working on cars and stuff."

"Your dad works as a mechanic?"

"Yeah. My mom works too. So I come here after school."

Timmy's chin began to quiver. "I just want to go home. The kids here make fun of me because of the mark on my face."

Betty worriedly glanced at the agents.

"Hey, we try to run a tight ship here," Betty said. "We don't allow any bullying."

"But Timmy was allowed to crawl up on the fence," said Audrey.

The co-owner couldn't look the two federal investigators in the eye.

"Hey, we've been understaffed lately—"

"What color were the clean overalls, Jimmy?" asked Kim.

"Blue. Not dark blue—I want to go home!"

"Are the parents en route?" Kim asked Betty.

"I think—"

"Hey, Jimmy, does your mother let you eat ice cream?" asked Audrey with a friendly grin.

"Yeah."

"How about we get you some ice cream and let you sit in our cop car? Would you like that? Just until your parents get here."

Jimmy's mouth almost formed a smile. "Sure."

Kim sat with Jimmy in her government Mustang and showed him all the bells and whistles as Audrey walked down the street to a Stop and Rob. She came back with an assortment of ice cream bars and cones. Timmy grabbed a fudge bar with a smile.

"The siren is cool," he said, biting into his ice cream bar.

"Yeah, it is," said Kim. "We get to chase around at the Academy in Georgia, sirens and lights on."

"Could I be an— an Agent someday?"

"Of course," replied Audrey as she joined him in ice cream. "You can be anything you want if you work at it."

"Even with this—*mark* on my face?"

"Yep," replied Audrey. "Heck, they let somebody as funny-looking as me in the FBI. Why wouldn't they let a handsome young man like you in?"

Jimmy laughed and attacked his fudge bar. Kim gave him an ice cream sandwich, promising not to tell his mom he had two ice creams. Jimmy added no additional details except Cat Mask screamed when Wendy stabbed the person with a pencil. His mother, Sandra Brown, arrived upset. She started yelling at Betty and Barney until Kim and Audrey distracted the young African-American woman.

Jimmy ran up and hugged his mother. "Can I take my son home?" his mother asked.

"Yes, Ma'am," said Kim as she watched Detective Fornier give her a 'yes' nod. "Please take our cards. Don't hesitate to contact us if Jimmy remembers anything else about the person who grabbed at him."

"They let me sit in the police car," Jimmy said with a grin.

"Thank you both," said Sandra. "I can see my son was in safe hands."

"We try," said Audrey. "Kim here is a mother now."

"First one?" asked Sandra as she held her son close.

"Fraternal twins."

"Ouch! Giving birth to this one was tough enough." Sandra kissed Jimmy's head. "I guess the EMTs gave him a check over and said he's okay."

"My friend Wendy was hurt," added Jimmy.

"We'll get her a card, maybe see her at the hospital. Thank you both again, Ladies."

"Anytime, Ma'am. Feel free to call us."

Sandra hugged her son as they walked to their car.

"Every mother's nightmare," said Kim. "Someone hurting your child."

"Shall we try to find Wendy at the hospital?" asked Audrey.

"Yep. Time to ask questions while the memories are fresh."

When Kim and Audrey arrived, Wendy's parents were at St. Joseph Medical Center. They hovered nearby as the ER Staff double-checked their young patient. Kim and Audrey introduced themselves as Barbara Watson, an older version of her daughter, and began talking.

"Wendy told us she stabbed some asshole who tried to kidnap her friend."

"It seems so, Ma'am," answered Audrey. "Your daughter is a tough young lady—and a bit of a hero."

The military-fatigued-wearing father, Greg Watson, smiled as he answered. "She takes after her mother. Toughest dental assistant around."

"This is not funny, Greg. Wendy has a concussion and some bruised ribs."

"Did she tell you anything, Mrs. Watson? About the person she stabbed."

"Just that he wore a cat mask and talked weird."

"You work at Joint Base Lewis McChord, JBLM, Mr. Watson?" asked Kim.

"Yes, Ma'am. U.S. Air Force Security Forces. I'm up for Technical Sergeant, E-6."

Barbara looked at her husband.

"I think, Greg, it's time to push for another

daycare slot on the base. We would have to arrange transportation, but it would be much safer.”

"Could we speak with your daughter?” asked Kim.

“I'd rather you didn't,” answered the father. “She may have to stay here under observation for a while due to the concussion. That is stress enough for one day.”

“Did she mention if the attacker was male or female?”

“Wendy said he was large like a man,” replied the mother. “The doctors chased me out after that.”

The two agents glanced at each other and gave a quick nod. “Okay, Sergeant and Mrs. Watson,” said Audrey. “We'll leave you with our cards. Call us when you think Wendy is up to some questions.”

“Why the interest from two federal agencies?” asked Greg Watson.

“Can't go into details right now,” replied Kim. “We are checking to see if it relates to other attempted kidnappings.”

“We'll call just as soon as Wendy is up to it,” said the father. “I have enough law enforcement experience to know what is left unsaid is as important as what is said.”

“Thank you both,” said Audrey. “We'll let you get back to your daughter.”

The agents shook hands and left. Greg Watson grinned.

“Why the grin?” his wife asked.

"We just met a local legend in police investigations."

"Who is that?"

"Agent Kupar, the one with the permanent tan? That is the Tiger Lady."

Detective Fornier phoned them and said he had a thumb drive copy of the daycare surveillance tape. The Special Agents met him back at the daycare.

"Don't expect much, ladies. They still use old VCR tapes over and over again."

Kim and Audrey returned to the HIS office and contacted Technical Agent Kelly Olivet. "Think you can play this and clean it up? It's from a beat-up VCR recording."

"Let me do my magic, Kim," Kelly said with a grin. The Technical Agent was a legend in the Northwest. Kelly was the man to contact if you had some electronic recording that needed work to make it usable.

Kim and Audrey went down to the chain coffee shop on the building's street level and obtained coffee for Kelly and Audrey and tea for Kim. A half-hour later, Kelly brought the thumb back with a frown.

"That VCR tape was crap. Some cheap bastards have recorded over it about a hundred or more times."

"Did you get anything?" asked Kim as she handed Kelly a coffee.

"Thanks. Come into my tech room. I have it on the

big screen."

Kim and Audrey watched a grainy and jerky recording of the young Jimmy climbing the fence. A blurry figure with an indistinct mask walked up to the chain-link daycare border and appeared to talk to the boy. Wendy then entered the frame and seemed to have a short conversation with the adult-sized figure. As the figure grabbed Jimmy, Wendy stepped forward and stabbed the attacker in the stomach. An automatic powerful mule kick sent Wendy falling back. Jimmy toppled from his perch and landed on Wendy as the figure took off running, holding its stomach.

"That young girl is wicked with that pencil," said Kelly. "Think we can get her on our team someday?"

"Maybe," replied Audrey. "Jimmy already expressed interest."

"Well, we see an adult-sized figure of what I would say is male proportions," Kim stated.

"Or a transgender woman," said Kelly. "Remember a certain former Olympian."

"You just like to complicate things, don't you?" Audrey said with a smile.

"Hell, I learned a long time ago I need to be exact as possible with electronic products. If you jump to conclusions on what you think you can see, some wise guy will tie you up in court, making you wonder if you have lying eyes."

"Thanks, Kelly. As Jimmy said, the images may be

blurry, but we have at least a specific-sized individual wearing coveralls. Can you try to clean up the face of the suspect? It should show a mask of some sort."

"Give me a few. I'll try."

Kim and Audrey went to Kim's desk and began to brainstorm. "So, we have a male, female, or transgender individual," said Audrey as she sipped her coffee.

"A suspect who is injured. We can put an APB out to the medical establishment to look for people with nasty puncture wounds to the stomach," replied Kim.

"Good thought, Kim. An individual might seek medical attention on their own. However, if a group of traffickers is involved —"

"They may have privileged access to medical aid. However, someone may panic and screw up."

"We can hope, Kim."

Kelly walked up to Kim's desk. "Here. Best I can do."

Kim and Audrey examined the blown-up image of the suspect's face. "Is that a cat mask, Kim?"

"Looks like it. Full face, maybe of film industry quality." Kim grinned at Kelly. "Excellent work as usual. Kelly."

"I aim to please. Just keep me in free coffee."

The two women stared at the image. "I hope that asshole gets sepsis from that pencil stab," said the FBI Agent.

"You and me both. You and me both, Audrey."

4.

alter Jenkins was on the run. He knew the Department of Corrections had a warrant out for him as he had failed to report in as ordered. That goddamned doctor! Murray just had to report him. All he wanted to do was tell everyone about those smiling kids he saw with those masked-up people. They all seemed so happy.

"Why can't I be happy? Don't I have a right?" Walter said to no one in particular as he walked down a back street in Tacoma.

Walter tried to reach where he had seen the kids and the masked people. In the excitement that day, he had followed them to an older former office building with all signage removed. Jenkins would have thought the building was abandoned if the group had not entered the building by a side door. A quick glimpse of the hallway revealed new carpeting and soft lighting. Then the adults saw him, brushed him off, and shut the door.

The overweight, balding Jenkins, with somewhat beady eyes and a goatee, stood in an alley and looked at the surrounding buildings in the older part of Tacoma. He took a deep breath and tried to relax. So many of the nondescript buildings looked alike in the waning daylight. Jenkins needed to locate that building before the Department of Corrections found him. Maybe, the mask people would allow him in if he could only convince them he had the children's best interests at heart. Jenkins just knew they would believe him.

He quickly glanced up and down the street and started walking again. The man had a mission.

It was another late night for Kim. The Twins were sound asleep when she arrived home. Once again, her loving husband Hank had the situation under control.

"I used your milk from yesterday's breast pumping, and now the twins are asleep with full tummies."

Kim kissed him and then tried to crush the herculean frame in a mighty hug.

"I don't deserve you, Hank."

"Yes, you do. Now sit while I make you some dinner."

"I need to pump some more milk."

"Well, do that while I make dinner for us."

An hour later, they snuggled in a loveseat near the twins' cribs. "So, anything new in the case?" Hank asked.

"A related kidnapping attempt thwarted by a young girl with a sharp pencil."

"I think I saw something on the local news about that."

"Well, we are hoping someone reports a wounded person," said Kim. "It would be nice actually to pin a kidnapper down."

"Think it is one or a group?"

"We don't know, Hank. Audrey and I lean toward an organized group. The kids just disappear, which is a lot for just one person to do. After all, until today, no suspect has been seen when the children are snatched."

Kim snuggled closer to her lover. "We hope surveillance tapes from my father's business may reveal a suspicious person. Audrey and I get to go frame by frame tomorrow."

"Well, don't exhaust yourself, Kim. You gave birth to the twins not that long ago."

Kim looked into her husband's eyes. "Imagine if it were our children missing. Would you want the people handling the case not to put forth their best efforts?"

"I would be out there with them, beating the bushes. But I also do not want a sick wife and mother on my hands when we have two children needing mother's milk."

Kim gave Hank a quick kiss. "I promise I'll not work myself to a frazzle. Since you're worried about my stamina, let's go to bed. The baby monitor is up and working, and I have plenty of breast milk in the frig. I'll give them breastfeeding in the morning.

Hank grinned as he spoke. "Just think if you had triplets. You would be one breast short."

"Nah. I'd make you take a lot of female hormones. Then you could help me out."

"I may have a large manly chest," replied Hank, "but the word *manly* is the operative term," he added with a laugh.

The two federal agents reviewed the numerous tapes obtained from the Kupar's business over the next two days. They revealed nothing, just the regular comings, and goings at a busy import-export company. Attempts to enhance the photos from the daycare revealed nothing new. A quick conversation with Wendy and her parents also provided no new leads.

And Walter Jenkins was still a no-show.

The only good news was there were no new abductions.

"No reports from ERs or medical clinics about treating a nasty stomach puncture wound?" Kim asked Audrey.

"None. The mystery Cat mask person is still

a ghost.”

Audrey's cell phone rang, and she answered it. “Agent DiStefano. Oh, Hi, Stan. What?“ She paused. “We'll be right there.”

“What's up?” asked Kim.

“They found a nude headless, handless, and footless body floating in the Puyallup River near the Port of Tacoma industrial zone.”

“You thinking what I'm thinking, Audrey?”

“Yeah. Someone who screwed up an abduction just got served.”

Kim used Code Three after Sector Control notified the Washington State Patrol that a vehicle would run lights and sirens towards the Port of Tacoma. The State Troopers were often anal about who could haul ass on *their* highways. Kim drove the Mustang to the Port of Tacoma office near the Puyallup River waterway in record time. They met Detective Fornier near the tarp-covered body on the river bank.

“You got the call, Stan?” asked Audrey.

“Yeah. I asked to be notified of any body calls. I felt that the person stabbed by that young girl would not be long for this world. People grabbing kids do not like publicly.”

“Good instincts,' said Kim. “Any idea about the identity of this body?”

“Nope. No tattoos to run in the system. The

Medical Examiner will check for the tell-tale pencil stab wound. Luckily, the body seemed to have only recently been dumped. It took some time for whoever did this to remove and dispose of the body parts."

"Any chance of a DNA match?" asked Kim.

"We can hope that John Doe was arrested and has a DNA sample in the system. However, that will take some time."

Kim knelt next to the body and looked under the tarp. "Hmmm. I guess that torso is about the same size as the blurred images in the video." Kim lifted the tarp as she stood up. She frowned as she examined the entire body. "Someone hacked out the entire genital area."

"Yep. Either someone was very pissed off or just wanted the ME to have more fun sex-typing the corpse."

Kim replaced the tarp. "We are dealing with some sick individuals."

"Yes, Kim," replied Audrey. "This points to an organized group trying to hide its tracks."

"I just hope the next body is not some innocent child." Kim looked at the Detective. "Can you call us when the Medical Examiner is finished?"

"You got it," said Stan."I'll keep my eye out for any missing child reports also."

"We owe you lunch," said Audrey.

Stan laughed and then replied, "Make it a stiff drink or two. I think we'll need it."

Reports of the mutilated corpse stirred increased interest in missing persons (including children) for a few days, then were pushed out of the public consciousness by wars, political fighting, and demonstration for or against the flavor-of-the-month. Kim and Audrey reviewed their information and pondered their next steps.

"Still no sign of Walter Jenkins," said Kim.

"I wonder if he will ever turn up. Alive, that is," replied Audrey.

"That body points to people willing to kill and dismember to hide their tracks," said Kim. "One less sex offender would not bother most people."

Audrey's cell phone rang. "Agent DiStefano. Hey Stan, what's up? No DNA matches in the system—I see. Well, thanks for all the effort. Keep in touch, and we still owe you that drink."

"No joy, as fighter pilots say."

"Right, Kim. There was evidence of wound probing right where Wendy would have stabbed the cat mask person."

"So it probably was Cat Mask. But we have no identification, no names, addresses, etcetera."

The two agents sat in silence until Audrey spoke. "You understand that we are looking for a highly organized group with a selective membership? "

"I agree. So I think we reach out to some civilian

non-profits dealing with human trafficking, like Polaris. They might have information from the shadows which has not reached law enforcement."

Audrey smiled as she answered.v"Two brains with a single thought. Nice."

"So, let's call it a day," said Kim. "We can start over again on Monday when the civilian offices are open."

"Hey, Kim, can I invite you to a workout at my dojo tomorrow? You can bring your better half and the twins. My Sensei would like to meet you and see some of your Indian martial arts."

"I could use a good workout," replied Kim. "I'll call you after I talk to Hank, although I think he would be glad to get out of the house with the kids. And he can meet you, Audrey."

"Yeah, I would like to meet the man who takes care of the Tiger Lady."

"One warning, Audrey."

"What's that?"

"You may be placed on a long list of potential babysitters, so I hope you like kids."

Hank drove the SUV as Kim sat in the back for face-time with the twins. The infants smiled and giggled from the matching car seats.

"I'll feed you two later," Kim said as she smiled at the literal fruits of her womb.

"Mommy has some things to take care of first."

"Just make sure you don't allow anyone to smash your breasts," said Hank. "The twins will not like an interrupted feeding schedule."

"I don't see a lot of full contact activity, Hank."

"Huh. It's a Karate dojo. Don't most dojos have full contact sparring?"

"My love, I'll handle it. I can still take care of myself."

"Always the Tiger Lady," Hank grumbled.

Kim realized Hank had been in a protective mood since he'd beat the holy Hell out of David Roskin and friends when they tried to grab a pregnant Kim. Despite his vocal support and taking the time necessary to care for the twins, Hank was still hesitant about Kim returning to work and now going to a martial arts dojo to work out. Kim knew the protective persona of a big cat senior male pride member was displayed in a hominid. However, Kim would not and could not be a shrinking violet of some old romance novel.

Hank parked the SUV in the Shorin-Ryu dojo parking lot. Kim and Hank removed the twins from their car seats and placed them in a special two-baby-carrying rig Hank had found. One was a baby pappose style on his broad back, the other in a protective carrier on his broad chest. Hank liked the protective feelings of both of his children close to his body. He swapped Rex and Lupe out, so each could view the various world views from front and back.

Audrey met them at the entrance wearing her karate gi. Kim saw she had a black belt wrapped around her waist.

"You did not tell me you were a black belt instructor."

Audrey shrugged as she answered. "I only went through the whole belt thing as it seems required in most schools. I took karate for the self-defense aspect, not the ranking business."

"My gurus, instructors, were more focused on my ability to perform the techniques than achieving a certain ranking," Kim replied.

Kim introduced Audrey to Hank and the twins.

"So this is the modern-day Hercules and large cat man," Audrey said with a grin.

"Guilty as charged, I guess," Hank replied with a smile. "Kim does tend to exaggerate."

"Hey, I read a certain police report. Talk about a senior male lion protecting his pride. Those intruders wished they had never met you."

Hank blushed as he answered, "Roskins and those assholes deserved it."

"No argument from me, big man. Now come on in, and I'll introduce you to Sensei Adachi."

Hank, Kim, and Audrey entered the dojo, bowing in a traditional respectful manner. A young black belt led the class of some dozen students through a complicated kata as a stocky, powerful-looking middle-aged man watched with a steady gaze. Audrey stopped the trio at the edge of the floor mats just as the middle-aged man yelled at the young men and women. The class froze in their last stance as the clearly identified sensei approached the young black belt first and then the other students. Short, crisp instruction in Japanese and English was reinforced with slapping arms into a corrected position or a foot sweep to show how off-balanced the practitioner was in the kata.

"That is Sensei Danuja Adachi," whispered Audrey. "He is very old school."

The Sensei finished his education in the class with low-volume chewing out of the young black belt. He then turned and walked straight toward the visitors and Audrey.

"Sensei Adachi, this is Kim Kupar and her husband, Hank," said Audrey as she bowed low. Kim copied the bow, as did Hank the best he could with two youngsters hanging on him.

"Ah, the Tiger Lady," said the Sensei with a grin. "And these two little ones must be yours. But I see no stripes or claws—"

"They are still young, Sensei," replied Kim. "Cubs often take time to grow."

Sensei Adachi laughed, then asked to hold each of the twins.

"Holding children as these bring back pleasant

memories of my younger years," the senior black belt replied. "My five children are away at school or married with children. I do not see my grandchildren as much as I wish."

Kim noticed Sensei Adachi spoke accentless English, which bespoke the fact he was U.S. born. She also saw he had a stern exterior as an instructor but concealed a soft heart.

"We are honored that you asked us to attend your dojo," said Hank as the Sensei returned the twins.

"It is not such an honor. Instead, I have a sneaky ulterior motive. Which I concealed from Audrey."

Kim asked with a raised eyebrow " And what is this hidden motive, Sensei?"

"My young students are not exposed to other forms of martial arts enough. They tend to become Okinawan Ryuku-centered; they think my teaching style is the best of all possible worlds. I wish to expose them to other ways of approaching the universe of combative systems."

Danuju Adachi grinned, adding, "And who better to introduce them to different styles and realities than the famous Tiger Lady."

Kim tried not to blush and failed.

"Hank, do you mind if I borrow your wife for a while?"

"As long as you don't bruise her," the large man replied. "She has Twins to feed."

"Don't worry, husband," replied Kim. "You know I can take care of myself."

"That does not make me worry less."

Kim addressed the Sensei.

"I wore traditional clothing similar to a karate Gi, as I thought you would want me to demonstrate some techniques."

"Thank you. Please allow me to organize my class for a demonstration."

Sensei Adachi turned toward the class, clapped his hands, and shouted commands. Within seconds the entire class sat cross-legged on the edge of the training mats. Danuja Adachi introduced Kim as she bowed to the U.S. Flag, the Sensei, and the mat area. The agent slowly walked to the center of the mat as the students watched.

"What do you plan to share with us, Tiger Lady?" asked the Sensei.

"Sensei, I will demonstrate the *kalarippayattu* version of the first karate *kata*. The formal name is *nerkaal meypayattu*."

"Hai! Now, everyone pays attention and learns. Shorin-Ryu may seem like the center of the universe to you in my class. However, these Indian martial arts are even older than what was taught in Okinawa." Sensi Adachi looked at Kim. "Please begin."

The Indian version of a kata started with some extensive low stretching. The leg stretching loosened Kim's hips and other joints for the signature high kicks in her martial art. She also stretched her arms and torso, with her hands often forming *sumaste* prayerful hands. Kim moved her arms and shoulders as if her hands were the head of a serpent. Many martial arts started with human attempts to copy animals' movements in the wild. Kalaripayattu was one of the first combat arts which incorporated such motions.

As Kim continued, she added extreme high kicks, then stretched low again while her hands formed blocks for possible attacks. The martial arts exercise ended with some combinations of slapping blows, kicks, and foot sweeps Kim added to demonstrate techniques of later *meypayattu*. Kim stood straight, then bowed to the Sensei with her hands in supplication.

"Sumaste," she said.

Sensei Adachi strode forward and bowed low to Kim.

"I sense you are the equivalent of a Black Belt in your art."

"I guess, Sensei. Knowledge of all the parts of Indian martial arts was more critical than ranking. Our Gurus taught humbleness in having skills over competing for rankings."

"Would you be willing to demonstrate some lite sparing with my senior black belt?"

"Sure, Hai! As long as it is lite—"

"Gou Higa. Front and center." Adachi's voice had the command tenor of one used for military orders and actions. Kim had not thought to delve into the background of Audrey's sensei and now wondered if she should have before accepting the invitation. Kim could not back out now without embarrassing Audrey and herself. Kim glanced at Hank and gave a hand sign of reassurance. The big man was already frowning in disapproval.

"All right. Gou—lite sparing. This is not a competition."

Kim and Gou bowed as the Sensei stepped over to Hank and Audrey. "Okay—if you are both ready, Hajime!"

Kim had assumed a low crouch defense considering the sparring would start to slow. She was wrong.

Gou exploded at her from a wide Shorin-Ryu stance with hard straight punches and low snap kicks. He was not holding back. Hank growled and started to step forward as Kim used her art's essential flexibility and mobility to slip to the side. She rolled out of the line of the attack and then put distance between her and Gou.

Sensei Adachi moved forward with Hank, and Audrey placed a lite hand on each as she stood between them.

"She can take care of herself. Watch."

Gou was surprised that Kim had slipped away from his attack so effortlessly. As he moved forward, the black belt raised his hands into a fisted boxing stance. Once again, Gou tried a series of straight punches and snap kicks. Similarly, Kim used avoidance techniques rather than blocks to stop the blows from landing. Frustrated, Gou went into a low and powerful leg sweep to show he could also be flexible.

Kim lept up, then somersaulted in the air. She landed behind a stunned Gou and dealt a signature open-handed slap to the side of Gou's head. Then Kim was once again yards removed from her opponent. Gou stood facing his opponent with a flushed face. Kim noticed for the first time that Gou seemed of mixed European and Japanese heritage. Maybe he had something to prove to the class, of which Kim had no clue. Kim glanced over at Hank and saw the twins were sensing their mother was not in a favorable state as they began to twist and fuss.

"Time to end this," Kim mumbled.

Gou let out a series of Kia's as he tried a bum rush to force Kim off the training mats. One second, his target was in front of him; the next, she was low and entangled her supple legs with his. Gou went face down as he tripped, catching himself with his hands. He twisted and reached a large hand out to grab Kim. Then, paralyzing pain shot through his body.

Somehow, Gou managed to slap the mat to signal he yielded. Kim helped him to his feet as the Sensei approached. "I think I have much to learn from your style, Kim-San."

"*Varma Kalai* is the knowledge of pressure points and the body structure," said Kim. "That knowledge can be used for hurt or healing. If the young man would allow me to help relieve the pain—"

"Please do," said Danuja Adachi.

Kim gave the young man a short massage, realigning nerves and muscles. As the agent completed the treatment, she noticed two female students were having trouble concealing their pleasure at seeing the young man at the mercy of a woman. Kim wished she could be a fly on the wall when the class went to the locker rooms.

Gou stood up and bowed low to Kim. "You are an excellent fighter," said the young man.

"As are you," replied Kim.

"So tell my class, Tiger Lady," said the Sensei. "What is the basis for your martial art?"

"Elegant and flexible movement, including evasions and jumps, are a staple of the art," answered Kim. "The ability to forcefully strike while using superior flexibility and mobility is also required."

"You are welcome to train here anytime you wish, Kim Kupar."

"It is an honor and a pleasure to be invited. Thank You, Sensei."

Sensei Adachi clapped his hands together and then bellowed loudly. "Pay homage and respect to this expert in the martial arts!"

The entire class stood up and bowed as one. Kim and Audrey bowed in return. Adachi then clasped Kim's hands in his own and, with a broad grin, said, "Go with God, my dangerous Tiger Lady. May your children grow tall and strong. Maybe someday they will return to train with me."

"That just may happen, Sensei," Kim replied with a smile.

Audrey escorted the couple and their children to their SUV, grinning ear to ear. "Now, that was a demonstration."

"That young man almost had a large fist in his face," growled Hank as he placed the twins in their car seats.

"My husband does not think I can take care of myself?" Kim asked with a mischievous smirk.

"That is not the point. The point is if someone hurts my wife and the mother of our children—"

"You will break them as you did those home invaders while I was pregnant."

"Something like that."

Kim wrapped Hank in a bear hug. "How was I so lucky to marry this modern-day Hercules? I do so love you."

"I'm insanely jealous," Audrey said with a broad grin. "Maybe someday I will find Miss Right."

"Hank and I will keep a lookout for such a person. Everyone needs a loving mate."

"I'll hold you both to that statement. Now, if you will excuse me, I need to return and train some more."

Moments later, Hank drove the SUV as Kim sat in the back seat and nursed her twins. "No damage to the twin's favorite meal tickets?" asked Hank.

Kim laughed. "No, my dear. My breasts were not battered."

"You know I worry when you put yourself in these situations."

"My love, you know I can take care of myself."

"You realize it is in a man's makeup to desire to protect his wife from harm."

"And you do an excellent job. However, I also must be able to protect myself in my line of work." Kim paused, then continued. "Both you and I were in danger around the big cats at the Zoo."

"They, I understand. In my estimation, my fellow nasty monkeys are much more dangerous than tigers and lions."

Kim smiled from the SUV's backseat. Once again, she realized the treasure she had in Hank. "I realize your concern. I promise I will be as careful as I can."

"Thank you," replied Hank.

"*However, I will still go where my job takes me, no matter the danger,*" thought Kim. She had her job. She would not do it half-assed.

5.

The two Agents met at the HIS offices on Monday morning. They then contacted the various civilian and non-profit organizations involved in human trafficking, abduction, and child sexual abuse. Unfortunately, none of them had any new information, even though they were well aware of the Rainbow Investigation, thanks to Amber Alerts, government contacts, and news reports. Thirteen missing Children of Color harkened back to the Atlanta Child Murders from 1979 to 1981 in the minds of some news outlets. The SAIC of the FBI was trying to keep a lid on that comparison. The Bureau had caught heat on their involvement from the media and some law enforcement officers.

"Audrey, The National Center for Missing and Exploited Children has no additional information or leads."

"Yeah, Kim. I hoped all the Amber Alerts on the thirteen missing children would turn up something new, some lead."

"The Polaris Project had no additional information either. "

"You know, Kim, they reminded us that most children abducted for sex trafficking are often groomed for abduction, often online. However, the young age of the victims, the oldest now seven, seems to preclude that idea. Kids are very tech savvy these days, but none of the victims had access to any electronic devices without the supervision of their parents."

Kim sipped at her now cold tea as she thought. Any attempt at brainstorming seemed to be fruitless this day. "Well, before we go and look for fresh tea and coffee, how about we call Bao Trang and see if Walter Jenkins turned up?"

"Sounds good to me."

Bao answered her phone on the second ring. "Officer Trang."

"Hey, Kim Kupar here on speaker phone. Audrey and I are brainstorming and are not coming up with new ideas or information. Any sign of Walter Jenkins."

"Sorry, Kim. There is a warrant out for his arrest for violating his supervised release. So far, he has not been at his usual haunts nor returned to the halfway house where he lives."

"Any more information from James Cannon?" asked Kim.

"No, although he was adamant about helping. Something you two said really lit a fire under him. I guess it was close to home."

"Thanks again, Bao."

"Anytime. A friend of my brother is a friend of mine."

Kim hung up the phone and looked at her partner. "Think Walter will show up alive—or as another floater."

"I'll bet you that if he contacts the mystery people he reportedly saw, they may decide to keep him from wagging his tongue," replied Audrey. "And that may be by cutting it out."

Baby Bear and Baby Fox called out commands to the other masked adults as they escorted the thirteen children to the dark-tinted windowed vans.

"Hurry up, people. It is time to go to the new safe location," said Baby Fox.

"I can't keep medicating the children like this," Baby Rabbit protested. "Keeping them happy is one thing. Making them into zombies is something else."

"If a *fool* such as that one can discover our secret place," said Baby Bear, "then the evil minions of the One World Government can also. That is why Baby Fox and I always have a contingency plan."

Baby Rabbit sighed, then replied. "I will do as you

wish. However, as a doctor, I must also think of the welfare of my patients."

Baby Fox stepped up and hugged the group's doctor. "And a fine doctor you have been. Soon, if the Lord wishes it, this will all be over. Then, we will tell the world how to keep their children safe. They have to listen—and obey."

"Thank You, Baby Fox. Now let me ensure all my patients are settled in the vans." Baby Bear watched Baby Rabbit walk away. Then, the masked bear person turned and walked into the adjoining room. Walter Jenkins was taped to a rickety wooden chair, creaking every time the prisoner shifted in his seat. Strong duct tape across the sex offender's mouth muffled his attempts at talking. Baby Bear stepped up and painfully ripped the tape from the prisoner's mouth.

"Ow!" Jenkins cried out.

"The pain you feel is your own doing, fool," Baby Bear said. "You should not have come looking for us."

"Please, I just want to help the children also. I mean them no—"

Baby Bear slapped him hard. "Shut up. Only lies come from your mouth. You are a sick pervert who wants to have sex with children. Your idea of helping is to force sexual relations upon some innocent child."

"No, you're wrong. I love childr —" Another hard blow stopped Jenkins in mid-sentence. He began to sob. Baby Bear stepped over, picked up a briefcase near the room entrance door, and opened it with practiced hands.

"This pistol was passed down from my Grandfather," said Baby Bear. "He was an OSS agent in World War Two. This High Standard HDMS, a twenty-two caliber pistol with an integral silencer, was a favorite assassination weapon, even in Viet Nam. My grandfather neglected to turn it in when he left military service."

"Please," said Jenkins as Baby Bear faced him.

"Let's see if it still works."

A bullet between the eyes silenced Jenkin's pleadings.

If Baby Bear removed the mask, an observer would see a self-satisfied grin. Since it stayed on, only the person under the bear mask knew of the grin.

"Time to leave, Baby Fox."

"The problem is taken care of ?" asked the Fox.

"Yes. Efficiently—and permanently."

Two more long days into the night, the Agents still had nothing new to show for their efforts. Audrey looked at Kim as she spoke. "You head home. I'll stay here and review some more of the weirdo files."

Audrey's records contained names and identifications of the worst of the worst of all types of abusers and pedophiles. A couple of unsolved 'Cold Cases' were included that involved missing children of the same age as the current victims. Audrey and Kim hoped something would spur them in a fruitful direction.

"That's not fair, Audrey. We share the late nights."

"Hey, lookit. You have two kids at home who need their mother, not her milk."

"That doesn't matter. We're both Agents—"

Audrey sighed. "Please, Kim. There is nothing that needs your attention here. Your Twins and your husband need your attention. Please, you can kick me loose early some night. Okay?"

"Oh, all right. You're as stubborn as I am."

"That's why we work together so well. We are both mules."

Only the porch light was on when Kim arrived home. She unlocked the front door quietly, stepped on the inner threshold, and set down her briefcase. The Agent balanced on one foot at a time and removed her shoes. Kim then tried to copy the stealthy stride of Sir Kahn as she made her way to the master bedroom. A slight snore told her that Hank was asleep in the padded recliner.

Kim peaked around the doorframe and smiled. Her human Hercules was asleep in the chair with the baby monitor clutched to his chest. The chair was situated so that if the monitor woke Hank up, he would immediately see the twin cribs. Kim blinked back tears at the sight of her steady and devoted husband. How was she so lucky to have rediscovered this almost-lost love after the disaster with John Wang? Not for the first time did Kim think it was a bout of insanity which caused the affair with a master criminal. Of course, she would never mention the idea of temporary insanity if she wished to keep her job.

Hank stirred in the chair, apparently sensing her presence. He turned his head towards her, opened his eyes, and smiled as he focused.

"The Tiger Lady returns to her cubs," Hank whispered.

"Let me get ready for bed, and I'll feed my twins," Kim whispered.

"No need. You pumped plenty of milk this morning. Your cubs both have full tummies."

"What did I do to deserve you, my loving lion, the leader of our pack."

Hank stood up and gathered Kim in his arms.

"So I am a male lion, a Mane, and you are a Tiger Lady. How did that happen?"

"Kismet, my love. Pure kismet."

They kissed long and deep until the baby monitor in Hank's hand told them the twins were stirring.

"Let me get ready for bed, Hank. Then I'll help you put the twins back to sleep."

"You need your rest, Kim. You are burning the candle at both ends. I can get the kids settled down."

Kim smiled, then kissed her husband quickly on the lips. "Deal. But I feed them in the morning. They need to know. Mom is still around."

"I promise. Now get to bed. Or I'll call you in sick tomorrow."

The night's sleep passed much too quickly for Kim. She did not want to give up the warmth of Hank's body next to hers. However, she must breastfeed the twins or pump some more milk. Hank was experimenting with mixing some baby formula. However, Kim was raised on her mother's milk and wanted to nurse as long as possible.

Kim still made it to work on time and was met by surprise in the building lobby. "Audrey. You beat me to my office." Her smile evaporated as she saw the serious look on her FBI partner's face.

"Let's talk in the coffee shop, Kim. Rear table, please."

Quickly, the two Special Agents claimed a table in the back corner, and each purchased their beverage of choice. As Kim sipped her tea, Audrey explained the frowns on her face. "I got a phone call from my big boss, the Assistant SAIC. They want to pull me off the case."

"What! Why?"

"As I said before. If the powers that be don't think the case is moving fast enough and catch heat from politicians and hard questions from the press, it's time to find a scapegoat."

"You're it despite what we have uncovered."

"An unidentified body of a person who could be

an attempted kidnapper. Then we have dead ends about who may be grabbing these kids and why. Yet, still, no recovered children." Audrey nervously slurped her coffee and continued. "The sick part is if a kid's body did turn up, then the FBI Lab could be involved; it would look like the case is progressing."

Kim patted Audrey's free hand. "Come on. We can go upstairs, and ASAC Weiss can make a phone call—"

"Hell no! Do you want the FBI brass to come unglued? Homeland Security telling them how to do their job? God, I'd be sent to Greenland on a special assignment just to get rid of me."

The two friends sat in silence as they finished their coffee and tea. Then Kim stood up. "Come on; We'll go to my office. No quitting until we're told to quit."

Audrey smiled. "You'd make a great Marine, always charging up the beach."

Kim chuckled. "My parents told me you quit when you are dead and with the spirits. Until then, you keep plugging."

As the two agents walked toward Kim's desk, Brenda, the SAC's secretary, headed them off. "Kim, ASAC Weiss would like to see you both in his office."

"Okay. Thanks, Brenda."

"It's been nice knowing you, Kim," said Audrey.

He was on his phone as the two women entered the ASAC's office. Tim Weiss motioned for them to shut the door and sit. Closing the door was a bad sign for Kim as it often led to ass-chewing in private.

"Remember that time, Marcia, and we were working that money laundering case in the strip club? Yeah, the one where the Group Supervisor wanted you to be a waitress there, or maybe even a stripper? Hey, I couldn't wear a garter belt and nylons; it was not a Gay strip club, now was it? Boy, did you chew that guy a new one and lecture him about sexual harassment—of course, it was funny, dammit. It would have been funnier if I had worn stockings with my hairy legs. Yeah, those were the good old days. Now it's all paperwork. So we have a deal? Yes, I owe you one now. Yes, I will fade the heat as I'm closer to retirement. And you still owe me a drink after work. See you soon, Marcia." Tim hung up the telephone and looked at Audrey, whose mouth was open.

"Yes, that was your Assistant Agent In Charge, Marcia Bernal. We met when I was a young U.S. Customs Agent, and she was a Task Force Officer in Florida. This case was before she joined the FBI and went to The Dark Side."

Tim Weiss looked at Kim. "You two have another week to come up with something. Then certain higher-ups will be looking for someone to blame."

"Pardon me, Sir, but how did you know the FBI was considering replacing Audrey?" asked Kim

"My spirit animal told me." The Homeland Security ASAC looked at Kim as her mouth fell open.

"Hey, you think you're the only one with animal contacts? Now, hit the road. I got you another week. Don't embarrass me."

As the two special agents walked out, Weiss called to Kim. "Agent Kupar, a quick word."

"Yes, Sir."

In a low tone, Tim Weiss said, "Do not work yourself into a frazzle. I will feel guilty as Hell that I put you back to work too early after having twins. You have unique investigative talents I don't want to lose. Okay?"

"Okay, Sir. And thanks. Audrey and I work well together."

"I know. My spirit animal told me."

Kim met Audrey back at the HSI agent's desk. A slight smile graced Audrey's lips as she handed Kim a cup of tea.

"Well, Kim, I have received a reprieve from my execution."

"We both have. If things go too wrong, I may be required to take some more maternity leave as an excuse for HSI to save face."

"Any ideas as to our next step?"

Kim sipped her tea as she paused in thought. Then a smile formed on her mouth.

"Want to take a chance and shake some trees to see what falls?"

"Go ahead, Kim. I'm up for most anything as long

as it is legal."

"I think it's time to use the Fourth Estate to our advantage."

"You have a media contact in mind?"

"Boy, do I ever."

6.

Rhoda Roberson was exercising at a local gym when her cell phone rang. She stopped lifting a substantial dead weight, wiped the sweat from her brow with her towel, and retrieved her cell phone. Rhoda had decided she might as well use her rather sizeable female frame to develop some extra muscle. The reporter had decided no one like David Roskin would ever again abuse her.

As Rhoda used her towel to push back her sweat-soaked brown hair, she answered, "Roberson here."

"Rhoda Roberson; Kim Kupar here."

The news reporter almost dropped her cell phone in surprise. She took a breath and then answered. "To say I am surprised to hear from you, Agent Kupar is an understatement. The reason behind this call must be unusual—and big."

"Can we meet somewhere? In Private?"

"*Bingo*," Rhoda thought as she answered. "You know *Fado's Irish Pub* on First Avenue? "

"Of course. Irish and cops go hand in hand."

"I'll meet you there in an hour. I need a shower first."

Rhoda walked into *Fado's* just over an hour later. As usual, the Agents sat at a table in the shadows of a secluded corner.

Kim stood up as the dark pants-suited reporter reached the table. "How are you, Rhoda?"

"Fine, Kim. Better than fine, as I know you are about to give me a major story."

Kim smiled. Law Enforcement and the Fourth Estate often had an acrimonious relationship. However, Rhoda and Kim survived a shared dangerous threat. Such situations often resulted in odd and lasting friendships. "Rhoda, this is FBI Special Agent Audrey DiStefano. They are the lead agency in this investigation."

"Huh. Things must be tight if the Bureau is willing to call in a reporter who is not afraid to criticize cops and the federal government in print."

Audrey smiled as she shook hands with Rhoda. "I'm a former Marine. We do what we have to do. Semper Fi."

"So, Agents? What's your poison? I hate to

drink alone."

After half an hour and some wine later, Rhoda looked at one agent and then at the other. "Everyone in the Media knew about the abductions, but we did not think they seemed so organized and connected. Not a random pedophile or serial killer, I believe."

"No bodies or recovered victims yet," responded Audrey. "At least not children."

"But you have an adult victim?" asked Rhoda.

"Not a real victim," answered Kim. "Rather, we think a possible co-conspirator who screwed up."

Kim laid out the details of the attempted abduction and recovered corpse.

"Sounds almost like a Mob hit, Kim. Russians, Albanians, Chechens, maybe, but not Italians. They lost control of this area a long time ago."

Audrey shook her head.

"No, Rhoda. Even the groups you mention would only grab kids for maybe a ransom or to force someone to work with them. And there would be more targeted kidnappings."

"Well, they are targeted in that they are all kids from minority populations. However, I have to agree that the chance of a criminal group grabbing kids from this many racial groups makes no sense. An organized pedophile group or human trafficking organization is usually less selective regarding diversity. They usually go after targets of opportunity, except for the fixation for young blondes in some parts of the world."

Kim smiled as she spoke.

"I told you Rhoda knew her stuff. Now, my Fourth Estate Friend, can you provide us some possible information sources we Feds don't have?"

Rhoda grinned. The Feds have to ask *her* for help—what a rush. "Give me a little time to work my magic. It has to be in private, of course."

"Of course. You have our numbers."

Rhoda threw back the rest of her wine, shook hands, and left.

"Is she good?" asked Audrey.

"The best at what she does. Which is snooping."

Kim was at home, watching the twins sleep as she readied for bed, when her cell phone rang.

"Agent Kupar. Rhoda—this is quick. What? Yes, I'll be there as fast as I can."

Kim kissed understanding Hank goodbye after throwing some clothes on. She arranged for a Seattle PD patrol car to pick up Audrey and met the FBI Agent at the jurisdictional border between Tacoma and Seattle. Waiting for Audrey to obtain an FBI vehicle from the motor pool wastes time. In Kims GOV, they followed a Tacoma-marked unit to an industrial area near the freeway overpasses interconnecting I-5 to Highway 16. Rhoda was waiting for them at the corner of two darkened city blocks.

"Whadda have, Rhoda?" asked Kim.

"This young lady here is Jewel. Let's say she is a—street worker."

Audrey and Kim saw a young woman barely out of her teen years with dyed bronze hair, a tight-fitting skirt, high heels, and sheer ripped black nylons. Jewel sucked a hit on a vape pen as she eyed the two Agents.

"Is this them?" Jewel asked in a husky voice.

"Yep. Now be nice. Kim is the Tiger Lady."

"No shit, Rhoda?" Jewel stuck a long-nailed hand out to shake. "You busting *The Jade Palace* helped free my current girlfriend from some massage parlor. She's going to dental college."

"And you're helping pay tuition," said Audrey.

"Yeah," said Jewel with a smirk. "Something like that."

"So what do you have, Jewel?" asked Kim.

"Walk with me, please."

The four women walked down the darkened street to a boarded-over door on the alley's edge. The building where the door was located had seen better days; painted-over windows on the street level and large old-style paned windows one story up.

"See this door? Boards are new."

"Which means—" began Audrey.

"Hey, no one wastes new boards on a shit hole like this. That is unless they don't want someone jimmying the door and finding something someone does not want to find."

"You know this area, don't you, Jewel," said Kim.

"Let's just say I've spent a lot of time—jogging around here, okay? This boarded-up door is new as of yesterday. And some friends saw some people loading kids into vans the day before yesterday."

The Agents froze for a moment.

"Kids?" asked Audrey.

"Yeah. Happy, smiling kids."

"Why not call sooner?"

"Hey, my friends said the kids were all laughing. Some had stuffed toys. Why screw up a fun time?"

"But you called about the door," asked Kim.

"Why use brand new boards if you leave a building you don't own? I—know the owner. He cuts us housing deals sometimes. You know. Then I saw the television and put two and two together."

"I managed to get a short report on missing children of color on the local news," interjected the reporter. "Someone owed me a favor."

"What did the adults look like?" asked Audrey.

"My friends said they were weird."

"How so?"

"They had coveralls or jumpsuits on, all the same color," replied Jewel. "And masks."

"COVID masks?"

"Nah. Holloween-type masks of animal faces."

Jewel helped the Agents locate the owner of the building and roust him from bed. Mister Hamza Sethi was a naturalized U.S. citizen from Pakistan who was none too eager to talk to federal agents.

Kim spoke some Pakistani, so she calmed him down. *"Sir, this is not about any—business arrangement you have with Jewel and her friends. This matter is about missing children."*

Hamza Sethi relaxed a bit and replied in English. "Would this have to do with the thirteen missing children mentioned on the news?"

"Yes, it would."

"Here, I will get a crowbar from my truck."

Using the crowbar, the owner and the Agents made quick work of the boards, blocking the door. Sethi then unlocked the deadbolts and opened the door.

"Hufffg. What is that smell?"

"Death," replied Kim. "Stand back." Kim and Audrey crossed the door threshold and tactically entered the building with flashlights and pistols. Audrey's light soon illuminated a seated figure at the back of a large room.

"Shit," said the FBI Agent. "Want to bet that bloated body is Walter Jenkins?"

"No," Kim replied. She called out to the two uniformed Tacoma cops who waited by the open door.

"We'll need Forensics and a coroner. Somebody died here."

It was a long night. Both Tacoma Homicide and the FBI sent Forensics Units to the scene. The teams soon discovered the entire first floor and basement had been swept clean. The owner also noticed some unusual modifications to his property.

"They soundproofed all the rooms," said Hanza Sethi. "I didn't authorize that work."

"Who leased this from you?" asked Kim.

"World Education Group. They provided me with references, incorporation paperwork, and credit checks."

"They paid cash also, I'll bet," said Audrey.

"Yes. But I have the groups bank account numbers, names of the senior managers—"

"We need to see all the paperwork. Now."

"I brought it. I thought it was strange the group left so quickly."

Kim and Audrey examined the documents as they talked with the owner. Sethi said the Neilsen Twins completed all the leasing forms and were the only members of the group.

"Identical twins?" asked Kim.

The owner shrugged. "They never referred to their gender, their sex. 'They' was used a lot in conversations. Nowadays, a landlord knows not to offend customers who pay cash by asking too many questions."

"But they looked the same?"

"They wore identical clothes, like jumpsuits and COVID masks that covered their faces, with hoods covering their hair. I thought they were paranoid about the Virus or were a member of a religion with strict dress codes. Some of my rigid fellow Muslims demand their wives and daughters are completely covered in public."

"Did you see any other group members?" asked Audrey.

"Yes. From a distance. These people were not twins and such but wore identical blue colored jumpsuits and overalls. They also all wore extensive medical face masks."

"How long ago did they move into the building?"

"Six months ago. They leased the entire building for a year but said they probably would not use all the space."

"Why lease the entire building?" asked Kim.

"The two said they wanted complete privacy. The building occupies half a city block, with a wide alley between it and the next building. I own that one also."

"Anyone occupies that building?"

"No. A couple of companies use it for storage."

"When was the last time you were here?"

The owner paused in thought, then answered. "Two months ago. I stopped by to verify the electricity usage. I work with the city to ensure no one is ripping off power for illegal drug-growing operations."

"But you saw nothing unusual? No children?"

"Why, no. This building is not zoned for some day-care operation."

"Well, it is now 'zoned' for a crime scene," interjected Audrey. "Don't expect to lease it again anytime soon."

"This is perfect," said Baby Bear. "I ask myself why we did locate here first."

"Because," replied Baby Fox, "we wanted an area closer to numerous families, daycare centers, schools, etc. We needed an area where children lived and played."

"True. Now, this secluded forested area will serve better for the next step of our mission."

"We have enough children?"

"Yes, The number thirteen also has a bit of an arcane connection, especially as Halloween is not that far in the future."

Baby Fox frowned under her mask. "Halloween is such a Godless day. Why it was allowed to flourish is beyond me."

"Because my dear Baby Fox, the Devil in all of us must sometimes act out. Halloween is a less deadly method for such an emotional release."

"Even though the One World Government makes use of such evil?"

"Why, yes. The mission will be completed when

we make our statement to the sheep of this country and the world. The message will be understood. The action we wish will be forced to occur—or else."

Baby Fox took Baby Bear's hand. "We have always had each other, yes?"

"We have always protected each other, Baby Fox. We had each other when others ignored the danger and the evil."

Baby Fox squeezed the companion's hand. "They will be forced to face what we faced. Now let us see how the others like it."

Walter Jenkins provided as little worth in death as he did in life. At least the Department of Corrections could close out its warrant for the violation of supervision. However, the two federal agents now had one less possible source of information. Forensics search of the area turned up little as the building had been cleaned by someone who knows police procedure.

Kim and Audrey watched the last forensic teams leave on the second day since the discovery of the body. The federal agents had little sleep since the discovery of Jenkins.

"Well, at least we know the people we are dealing with are not just some random nutjobs," Audrey opined as she sipped her cold coffee.

"Nutjobs may be sloppier and leave more evidence. However, I will admit that we would probably be finding children's bodies by now if sick pedophiles and child rapists were involved."

"Kim, did Rhoda come up with any more associates of Jewel to interview?"

Kim shook her head as she spoke.

"Nope. The limited descriptions of the children and adults are all we have. However, since a couple of Jewel's co-workers said at least two were children of color, I am sure this was our group."

The two agents stood silent until Kim said, "I think you need that coffee warmed up."

"I agree. Even with a rush job, filing all the forensics reports will take a day or two."

"Come on, partner. I know a particular Chinese Restaurant where we can have fresh coffee and tea and privacy.

7.

T*he Jade Garden* had a lull in afternoon business as the agents arrived. When the owner, known far and wide as Mother Bao, saw Kim, she called out and made a beeline to her. A motherly hug and rapid-fire Mandarin Chinese made Audrey grin. This woman had adopted Kim as another daughter, it seemed. Mother Bao switched to English when she finally let go of Kim and addressed the FBI Agent.

"You work with Kim?"

"Yes, Ma'am."

"Call me Mother Bao. Everyone else does."

"This is FBI Special Agent Audrey DiStefano. I am working and investigating with her."

"The missing children, yes? All my staff and friends are keeping their eyes and ears open. Someone who takes children is—"Mother Bao used an obscene Mandarin term that made Kim blush.

"Here, have your table in the back, Kim. And bring your children to the restaurant. Everyone here wants to see them."

"I promise, Mother Bao."

"Now, tea and coffee, yes?"

Kim and Audrey sipped their beverages and munched on fresh rice cakes and pastries. "Well, Audrey, any ideas about what we do next?"

"Well, I suggest we expand our search area. I bet the group who took the children have relocated well out of the Seattle-Tacoma area."

"Why do you think that?"

"I have this gut feeling they know someone is on to them. The media coverage Rhoda arranged after the discovery of the body would be a big tip-off to an organized group."

Kim sipped her tea as she considered Audrey's comment. "You know, I have to agree. Then the next question is to locate where? Traveling with a group of kidnapped children would not be easy if I wanted to disappear. So, do I move them someplace hidden nearby but outside the Seattle-Tacoma metroplex? And where would that be?"

Audrey grinned. "Where did a huge feline escape when you and others were looking for him?"

"Why, across the Narrows Bridge. So you think—"

"Out in the boonies of Kitsap County. Hell, if a modified tiger can hide within spitting distance of human communities for months, an organized human group should have no problems slipping into the area."

Kim grinned back at her investigative partner. "No rest for the wicked, Audrey. Guess who gets to review the hours of the Washington State Department Of Transportation Tacoma Narrows Bridges traffic cameras?"

Baby Bear sat looking at the acres of wooded property they now occupied. The long back porch of the grand old house near the Olalla area was a comfortable and relaxing place to sit, observe nature, and think. Baby Bear and Baby Fox purchased the property when discussing The Plan. That seemed like ancient history, even though it was just a few years prior.

Baby Rabbit's footsteps on the older wood porch interrupted the reverie. "Yes, Doctor?"

"The children are all resting in their new beds, Baby Bear."

"Thank you. The trip here was stressful. I am glad the children are enjoying their new home."

"You and Baby Fox built this house and connected buildings. They are so much nicer than the building we just left."

Baby Bear stood up and faced the doctor. "Yes, we built up this location just before and during the beginning of the Pandemic, as it is called. Cash-strapped small local construction workers were more than happy to finish this retreat, as I call it, without Kitsap County licenses and paperwork. Thus, the diagrams and layout of this property and structures are not on file."

"Don't the tax assessors come by and check?" asked Baby Rabbit.

Baby Bear smiled as he spoke. "That is why we concealed the larger portion of it underground. Building the basements and underground shelters away from prying eyes in this wet climate took money and skill. However, what are money and sweat when performing a noble mission."

Baby Rabbit hugged the bear-masked figure. "You have indeed performed a righteous act. It is an honor to work with you."

"The feeling is mutual. Now, let's check on our charges. We must ensure they stay healthy and happy." Baby Bear's face behind the mask clouded over. "They must be safe and happy, unlike what we suffered in the outside world."

Kim and Audrey spent a long day reviewing the Tacoma Narrows traffic camera footage. Then they managed to obtain the help of a young HSI Intern on a work-study grant. Georgina Teller was a great help in relieving eyestrain. On the second day, they received a lucky break.

State Trooper Susan Etheridge called the HSI office and asked for Kim. Susan had been one of the persons who saw Sir Kahn escape into the forests of Kitsap County, which led to his foray into the Olympic Forest.

"So, how is the Washington State Patrol treating you?"

"Just fine, Kim. I still get kidded about a large, unusual feline almost knocking me on my butt."

"Yes, he made a definite impression, Susan. Now, you have some information about some white vans you saw."

"Yes. There is a Park and Ride off Highway 16 at the Mullenix exit. I drive through it and check for people trying to steal parts or gas from parked cars. I saw three white stretch vans with dark-tinted windows parked in one row with kids walking around them. I drove by them, and two drivers wearing Covid masks and blue jumpsuits waved at me. I might have made the mistake of assuming they were some church or school group, although, in my defense, the children I saw were standing around with soft drinks."

"You wouldn't know who they were," interjected Kim. "Hell, we still really don't know who they are."

"Well, I live in the neighborhood, so I'll keep an eye out. They may have been passing through."

"Thank you. We'll stay in touch."

Audrey pulled some photos and papers from a

working case file. "Our Intern found some white vans on the DOT videos crossing the Narrows Bridge onto the Peninsula. However, they were all traveling singularly, not in juntos."

"Want to bet, my FBI friend, that these people are smart enough to know people are watching?"

"So, Kim, they do not travel in a convoy to attract attention. Your Trooper friend stumbled on them all bunched up by sheer chance."

"Let's review the time stamps on the photos of the vans. I bet you they are well-spaced."

"What is the bet?"

"You buy today's lunch, Kim."

Later, the two agents chowed on classic beef burgers at a local burger joint, Kim's treat.

"I would have thought you are more of a vegetarian from your East Indian heritage, Kim."

Kim laughed over a mouthful of Dick's double beef burger. "You forget my mother is from Argentina. She would have disowned me if I had refused to eat Argentine beef. My father knew her desire for meat going into the marriage."

"And yet they worked it all out."

"True love conquers all, Audrey."

"Like you and Hank."

Kim paused in her meal and looked at her investigative partner. Then she answered. "You probably already know about my problem with a local Chinese businessman."

"A certain businessman who became a meal for a special large cat," replied Audrey.

"Now is the time for brutal honesty; I thought John Wang was a true love. And my passion did not change the fact he was an evil man. No matter how much love there may have been between us, it would never change the fact he was a murdering swine."

Audrey paused before speaking. "That was hard to admit, wasn't it?"

"If I wanted to continue being a federal agent, I had to admit my serious fuck-ups."

"But you didn't have to admit it to me, Kim."

"Yes, I do. We are about to get all tooth and nail with a secret organization that kidnaps kids and chops up adults. If we don't completely trust each other—"

"I've got your back, Kim. We are simpatico, as they would say, on the Southwest Border. The Marines taught me that no one is perfect." Audrey took a sip of her soft drink. "But when the fecal matter hits the rotating blade, we're all Marines."

Kim grinned. "My Training Officer Moyer told me that sometimes you must take a big bite of a shit sandwich to get things done. It's better when someone helps you eat and enjoy it."

Audrey laughed long and hard. She finally stopped and wiped tears from her eyes. "Are you sure you weren't a Marine in another life?"

"I don't think so. But as people say, only God knows."

Audrey jabbed a French fry into a pool of catsup. "Well, if we put catsup on the sandwich, it may taste better."

The rest of the people at Dick's Drive-In looked at the two crazy ladies laughing up a storm and moved several feet further away,

Early the following day, Kim and Audrey examined civilian and government satellite photographs of the Olympic Peninsula at the HSI office. Kim thought that after Sir Kahn was no longer around, she would not be spending time on the Western side of Puget Sound. Now it appeared she was mistaken.

"Lots of trees and rural houses," Audrey stated.

"Which will make it difficult if they keep the children secluded," Kim replied.

"I guess FLIR wouldn't help much as there are already many people and large animals around."

"True, Audrey. It's not like a military operation over a desert. We had a Hell of a time trying to track Sir Kahn. Hmmm."

"What's the 'hmmm' about, Kim?"

"A particular modified tiger hid in caves. I wonder if there are any caves or old underground structures around Kitsap or Mason Counties."

"I guess we need to contact the county courthouses and offices to see if they know of any old structures or new homes with large basements and cellars. Thirteen kids will not be easy to hide."

"Unfortunately, I see a lot of traveling time in our future. I'll tell ASAC Weiss we'll spend time in our Tacoma Office area of responsibility."

"I'll check with my supervision. I see some late nights, Kim. We have a large area to cover."

Kim sighed. "The body of Walter Jenkins lit a fire under local law enforcement. There is talk of creating a task force based on what we uncovered. Everyone knows the investigation involves an organized group, not just one or two nutjobs."

"Well, shall we hit the road before we have dozens of boots on the ground, stomping all over the place?"

"Might as well, Audrey. I'll introduce you to a Texas-style barbecue place in Gig Harbor I found. The brisket is to die for."

"I'll hold you to that promise."

8.

Rebecca Richards drove along one of the side roads of Olalla, Kitsap County, as she tried to keep an eye in the rearview mirror. In the back seat were her Twins, Jack and Jill. Between them sat Snow, a huge white-furred dog of unknown parentage. Snow and her equally sizeable black mate, Blackie, had come to the Richard family household under very unusual circumstances. However, they were family members now, so raven-haired Rebecca kept a lookout that the twins did not feed Snow all the fresh apples she was delivering to a local homeowner. Orchard House, the Richard family's home, lived up to its name with many fruit trees. Rather than waste the bounty, Rebecca shared it.

"All right, you two. Snow has had

enough apples."

"We have plenty, Mom," replied nine-going-on-nineteen Jill.

"And Snow has had plenty. Now mind your—"

Snow suddenly voiced a loud growl and started for the front seat. "Whoa, Girl! What's up?"

Snow and Blackie were sensitive to the unusual to an Nth degree.

Snow's muzzle was up against the windshield as Rebecca braked the SUV. She looked in the direction Snow's muzzle was pointing, "What the Hell—"

Marching down the opposite of the road was a four or five-year-old dark-skinned little girl. She had her head down, and her hands clenched into little fists as her tiny legs motored her—somewhere.

"Hang on, kids," Rebecca called out as she drove the SUV to the opposite side, facing traffic. "Screw any tickets," Rebecca said, adding, "You two stay in the car. No arguments."

Jack and Jill recognized Mom's Command voice, so they knew not to bicker.

The former fighter pilot opened the door and exited the SUV in a flash.

"Hey, little girl, what's the hurry?" The dark-haired girl noticed the SUV and Rebecca for the first time.

"I want my Mommy!" she said as she stopped a few feet away from Rebecca.

"Well, let's see about finding her. What's your

name, honey?"

"Grette. I want my Mommy!"

A massive male figure in a blue jumpsuit stepped out from roadside bushes fifteen yards away.

"Grette! Come back here!"

Rebecca noticed the man was built like an NFL lineman, wore an N-95 facemask, and was not of Grette's ethnic background, nor looked anything like someone's mother. The retired combat pilot slid her hand to the small concealed .380 AMT BackUp pistol in her waistband. She'd try for a headshot on such a massive individual if it came to that.

"Pardon me, sir, but what relationship—"

"I would mind my own business," the man snapped as he strode towards the little girl.

Rebecca was drawing the small pistol when a large white shape flashed past her as Snow entered complete protection mode.

The colossal canine slammed into the stranger like a linebacker at the Superbowl. The man yelped as he tumbled into a small roadside ditch with Snow on top of him. The dog latched her teeth onto a bulky bicep, and the screaming began.

"Snow! Out!" Rebecca yelled as she noticed a second and much smaller figure emerge from the roadside trees further down. A Halloween-style mask covered the face of this new person.

"Time to leave. Snow. Out!"

Snow bounded back into the SUV as Rebecca snatched up the young girl and shoved her toward Jack and Jill.

"Hold on to her, tight," Rebecca commanded as she reversed the SUV. The former combat pilot managed to haul ass backward down the country road for a good half-mile before performing a Bootleg Turn her retired Pararescue husband had shown her. Jack and Jill squealed in enjoyment at their mother turning a car into a carnival ride. Now driving forward, Rebecca hit the speed dial 911 on her cell phone.

"9-1-1 Operator. Is this an emergency?"

"Damn straight. I just broke up a kidnapping on County Road...."

Baby Bear was incensed as he watched Baby Rabbit patch up the torn arm of Baby Gorilla.

"How did Grette get into the back of your vehicle?"

"I don't know!" said Baby Gorilla as he winced in pain. "I didn't notice her until I was miles from here and stopped at a four-way stop. Somehow the little brat—"

Baby Bear jabbed the mangled bicep with a wooded twelve-inch ruler. The massive man yelped. "Do not insult the children."

"Ask Baby Raccoon why she overlooked Grette until the little kid opened the van's back door. I was driving, and she was just a passenger."

Baby Bear slapped the ruler hard across Baby Gorilla's face. "Do not refer to your group mate by gender-restrictive terms. The less we give away to society's identity cult, the fewer chances we will be tracked."

Baby Bear stared at Baby Rabbit. "I thought you had them under chemical control."

"I can't keep them zoned out all the time. That will turn their developing minds into mush."

Baby Bear grumbled under his breath. "Finish patching Baby Gorilla up. I need to talk with Baby Racoon."

Baby Bear met Baby Racoon at a small office in the underground complex. "Why did you wear your special mask where the Outsiders could see?"

"I just grabbed it when Grette ran from the van. I'm sorry, Baby Bear."

"We are not ready for the world to know of our Mission. Your mask is for use only with the children and around our compound. Outsiders will not understand who or why we exist. Remember that and be careful next time. Mistakes at this late date must not happen."

Baby Racoon hung her head and sobbed.

"Oh, go to your sleeping quarters! And think about what you may have done."

Baby Bear met Baby Fox at the large common area where the remaining dozen children were being kept busy with educational games and play. They had been well fed for the night and would soon be sent to bed in the Sleeping Circle. Individual beds were in a large circle, with one of the adults in the center keeping watch.

"How could Grette sneak into the van?" asked Baby Fox.

"Our members must be getting so lax that they did not miss her. Grette may be small, but she is not invisible."

"Everyone is tired and fatigued from the forced move," said Baby Fox.

"Then we all must work harder and force ourselves to be alert. We are at the juncture of critical actions. Our Mission *must not* fall apart now."

Baby Fox took Baby Bear's hand. "We will get through this time of stress and conflict—together. As we always have."

Baby Bear grinned under his mask. "Yes, We survived together. And now, we must force the world to change. No child should ever have to—survive as we did."

The two Originals hugged. When the siblings were together, all seemed right with the world.

Kim was breastfeeding her twins when her cell phone rang.

"Hello, Kim here," she answered via speakerphone.

"Kim, Weiss here. Sorry, but it's all hands on deck.

In your investigation, we just had a major break fall in our laps."

"What happened?"

"Grette was just found in Kitsap County—alive and well."

Once again, Hank had to take over caring for the twins as Kim rushed out the door.

"You be careful, Kim."

"Always, my love."

Tim Weiss arranged a meeting with the FBI and State and Local agencies at the HSI Resident Agent In Charge Office in downtown Tacoma. It had a sizeable secure conference room that would allow all law enforcement to discuss the sensitive investigation. Kim was also told that Grette's parents would meet her there. Tim Weiss wished her to interview Grette to ascertain if the little girl could provide helpful details. The rescuer also volunteered to come to the office and review the details of her finding Grette.

Kim walked upstairs to the RAC office. As she reached the entrance hallway, she heard a young cry. The next moment a young boy had his arms wrapped around her.

"I told them the Tiger Lady would find my sister!"

Kim looked up and saw Bahadur's parents, Brigette and Balvir Jaswal. And behind them walked Audrey, escorted by a raven-haired woman and the largest snow-white dog Kim had ever seen.

"Bahadur, I think the person who found your sister is approaching us."

"But without you, Grette would not have been found. The spirit of Durga is in you!"

Balvir and Brigitta stepped up and untangled the young boy from Kim as Audrey grinned behind them.

"I have someone to introduce, Kim," said the FBI Agent. "This is Snow and her human, Rebecca Richards. They are the ones who found Grette."

"Where is Grette?" asked Kim as the white canine padded straight toward her.

"We have her being checked out by EMTs and a Forensic Psychologist from the Special Victims Unit. So far, she seems well-fed and healthy."

The rest of the conversation was interrupted as a large white canine rose and placed its paws on Kim's shoulders. Snow looked directly into the Special Agent's eyes as Rebecca Richards yelled, "Snow! Get Down!"

"*Sir Khan*," Kim thought as she locked eyes with this unique dog. Behind the eyes was a similar exceptional intelligence, and Kim felt lonely and lost.

"I am so sorry, Ma'am," said Rebecca as she reached out for Snow. "She doesn't usually jump on people."

"She's the Tiger Lady!" Young Bahadur blurted out.

"Oh. I never put the name together with—Kim

Kupar. You are a bit of a legend on the Peninsula."

"But you and Snow found Grette, not me," Kim replied, scratching Snow's ears. "You will be heroines now."

"Nah. We just stumbled onto something and did what we had to as responsible beings." Rebecca grinned as she watched Snow enjoy the ear scratching. "You have a way with beasties, and Snow has a new friend."

"She seems—unique," replied Kim.

Snow finally sat back down on her four paws. Then she padded over and nudged Bahadur, who gave the K-9 an enormous hug as his parents approached Rebecca. Birgitta hugged Rebecca as the mother of Grette held back tears.

"Thank you and your dog for returning my baby," she said. "We will be forever indebted."

"As I said, we just did what was necessary. The rest was pure chance."

"We'll need to debrief you some more, "interjected Audrey. "This is the biggest break we have had in the investigation so far."

Tim Weiss stepped into the hall and motioned to Kim and Audrey. "Sorry to interrupt, but we are about to start a briefing. I'll have Georgina, our intern, find a room for you and some refreshments. Grette is on her way to this office with the Forensic Psychologist.

"Thank you, sir, for all you have done," Balvir said as he stepped up and shook the ASAC's hand.

"Just doing our job, sir. Please excuse us. Agents, this way, please."

Inside the conference room, FBI ASAIC Marcia Bernal stood behind the podium in the front. This case was still a primary FBI investigation, so they took the lead. Representatives of various Federal, State, and Local law enforcement agencies were scattered around the room in chairs and at a long table. Macia saw Kim and Audrey as they entered and motioned them to the front of the room.

"Shit," said Audrey under her breath. "I do not want to be the center of attention."

"Could I have your attention, please," said the FBI supervisor. "This will be quick and dirty tonight as we have a lot of work ahead of us."

Bernal paused, then continued.

"FBI Agent DiStefano and Homeland Security Agent Kim Kupar are the lead investigators on what is now becoming a Task Force Investigation. Your respective agencies assigned you in this room to what is now the Operation Rainbow Abduction Task Force. Some of what has happened has hit social media already. We can expect a lot of commentaries as well as both good and bad leads. The bottom line is tonight, thanks to a concerned citizen, we have recovered one abducted little girl."

Marcia paused for a moment, then continued.

"However, we still have a dozen missing children, the oldest seven years of age. Thus, we hit the ground running. I will now put the two Agents on the spot by having them come forward to brief you on what they know and to answer any questions." The FBI ASAIC paused once more. "Remember one thing. An organization is involved, unlike a typical trafficking conspiracy or a pedophilia group. Thus, think outside the box, as these—miscreants have killed and have been one step ahead of us. Now, I turn it over to the Co Case agents."

"Senior agency goes first," whispered Kim.

"Thank you fucking much," Audrey whispered back.

Kim and Audrey managed to keep their briefing short and to the point. Grette had been recovered close to a boundary between Pierce and Kitsap Counties, so there were two Sheriff's departments involved in addition to State Patrol, local police, and additional personnel from the FBI and ICE. Weiss and Bernal organized individual assignments and shifts to free Audrey and Kim to interview Rebecca and Grette. The two Agents needed to ascertain how close the other kidnapped children could be to where Grette was found.

Grette sat on her mother's lap as she told Kim and Audrey about their existence during the last couple of weeks.

"Baby Bear and Baby Fox made sure we had food and toys," the young girl said. "Baby Rabbit was a doctor and checked to see we were all okay."

"So, everyone was friendly?" asked Kim.

"Yes. Baby Fox had all the other helpers watch us and ensure we played together nicely. They played games with us. It was fun." Then a cloud passed over Grette's face. "But I missed Mommy. And Daddy. And my Big Brother." She hugged her mother. "Sorry I scared you, Mommy."

Her mother tried not to cry as Audrey added, "Hey, you didn't scare her. The people who took you made her afraid, not you."

Grette smiled. "I like you. You're nice like the helpers were."

"How many helpers were there, Grette?" asked Kim.

The little girl sat in concentration momentarily, then held up two hands with spread fingers. "This many. I think."

"So, at least ten."

Grette nodded her head. 'Yes.'

"Did they all wear masks like Babby Bear, Baby Fox, and Baby Rabbit?"

"A huh."

"Who took you from the playground?"

"Baby Clown did."

"Was Baby Clown a boy or a girl?".

Grette paused in thought for a moment, then answered. "I don't know. I saw the mask; it was funny, then I fell asleep."

"Did anyone hurt you—scare you?"

"Only Baby Gorilla when he chased me after I jumped from the van. Then Snow came and saved me. Mommy, I want a dog like Snow."

Birgitte blinked back tears and hugged her daughter. "We'll see," she said.

"Do you remember the van ride to the woods?" asked Audrey.

"The car windows were dark, and the helpers had us sing songs on the trip."

"What kind of songs?"

The little girl paused in concentration, then began to sing. "The ants go marching one by one, hurrah—"

"Hey, I used to sing that one," replied Audrey.

"You did? You took trips as we did?"

"School trips, yes. But in buses, not vans with dark windows."

"Baby Bear had everyone stop and gave us all some drinks. Then I was tired and fell asleep. When I woke up, I was in a new bed."

Grette looked at her mother. "Mommy, can I go home now? I'm tired."

Kim smiled as she answered. "That is a good idea. You have been a very brave girl and gave us lots of good information."

Grette giggled with glee, then asked, "Can I hug Snow again?"

"Let's go ask her."

Rebecca sat patiently in the next room with the large-than-life white dog. Snow went directly to Grette when the little girl squealed her name.

"Methinks Snow has a new friend for life," said Rebecca Richards with a grin.

Grette gave Snow a big hug; her mother lifted her up. A teary-eyed Birgitte thanked Rebecca once again.

"De nada," replied Rebecca. "I have twins at home. You would do the same for me if you thought Jack and Jill were in danger.

"Our family still owes you a great debt," said Birgitte. "You are welcome in our home anytime you wish." With that, the grateful mother left and joined her husband for the trip home.

"One down and twelve to go," said the FBI Agent.

"Yes, Audrey," replied Kim. "Thanks to Rebecca, the search area has been reduced."

"Hey, as I said. You would both do the same if you saw a little girl alongside the road. Besides, Snow saw her first."

"Can we bother you with another review of maps and satellite photos?"

"Of course. Snow here would not let me leave if there is something more to be done, would you,

Big Girl?"

Kim thought for sure he heard Snow in her head answer, "Of course."

As Rebecca looked over photos and maps, the forensic psychiatrist Charles Brown conferred with Audrey and Kim. The FBI used Doctor Brown's skills in previous investigations and he knew Audrey. Kim saw he walked with a limp and wondered about the history of his injury. As she looked closer, Kim noticed his left hand was replaced with a hook.

"Agent Kupar. Please to meet you. Your reputation precedes you."

Kim smiled as she shook his good hand. "Don't believe everything you hear." Kim continued.

"So, any signs of abuse after interviewing and examining Grette?"

Charles slowly shook his head. "That is the weird part. Grette was kidnapped and yet lived in a family-like situation. She is healthy, well-fed, and seems to have made some friends. She remembered a few names of the other children, which I'll list in my report. They match names on the list of missing children of color you gave me."

"So, no indication of any injuries, bruises, mental problems—"

"Further blood work will be more specific, but Grette seemed to be kept happy with various sedatives and medications. Eventually, good old homesickness and missing her family outweighed any happy pills. So, she snuck into a van to try and find Mommy."

"And some guardian angel helped her be at the right place and time to be found."

Charles laughed. "I think a four-legged furry angel did the trick. I met Snow. She sensed something was wrong."

"Now we have to try and figure out how far Grette traveled from the concealed location," Kim said.

"The little girl told me she was in a large basement or underground room," replied the forensic psychologist. "Someone left a door ajar, and she went outside. It sounds like whatever medicine or drugs were being used to control her weakened in its effects."

"The entire Olalla and the connected Gig Harbor area is forested," replied Kim. "And, quite a few historical homesteads and farm plots scattered about the area. New underground construction or modification of root cellars will require extra investigation to connect the dots."

"If there is anything else I can do to help, let me know," said Charles. "I'll review my tape recordings and complete a written report ASAP."

"Thank you. Grette is the first real break in this investigation."

The two Federal Supervisors arranged for the FBI, Homeland Security, State, and County law enforcement forensic teams to scour the area where Grtte had been found. Kim and Audrey were the on-scene Case Agents, so all possible evidence recovered could be perused in real-time before submission to the various crime labs. Some long white canine hairs were found and appeared to match Snow. This discovery helped solidify Rebecca Richard's memory.

"Thank God we had a trained military pilot on the scene," said Audrey. "Her attention to location detail made this initial pinpointing possible."

"Yes, Audrey," Kim said as she sipped another hot tea. Audrey had a matching cup filled with barista-prepared coffee. "However, we still have dozens of square miles of woodlands to search. I guess it is too much to hope we find some human blood from the results of Snow's bites."

"Well, no rest for the wicked. How are Hank and the twins holding up?"

Kim smiled. "They are all troopers, although they miss my breastfeeding. Thank God for modern breast pumps."

"I think I may forgo the experience of childbirth and milk producing," replied Audrey with a grin. "Maybe I will find a partner who wants to be the mommy."

"We'll start a forensic and investigative search for just that type of woman after this ends."

"You'd do that for me?"

"Why should I have all the fun of marriage,

Audrey? Share the wealth is my motto."

An FBI Forensic Agent walked towards the two Case Agents while talking on a cell phone. He hung up just as he reached them.

"The canine clumps of hair match Snow," said the Forensic Agent. He grinned as he continued. "And a clump seems to have human blood on it."

"Bingo!" Audrey stated. "There is God for cops."

Baby Bear angrily slapped a copy of the *Kitsap Sun* newspaper onto a conference table. "Grette's recovery has thrown a real monkey wrench into our Mission."

Baby Fox walked up and patted a shoulder.

"We will get through this, Baby Bear. The One World Government has no records of our staff, the Helpers. We were careful in our selection. Only you and I are—in the system."

Baby Bear's face flushed. "And that is what started this all. The 'system' is what led us to this point. No system, no need for our Mission."

"We have been off the radar, as they say, for years. We have used valuable surrogates in almost all our dealings. Thus, our cash and our wealth are well hidden."

Baby Bear sighed. "You were always the calm one, Baby Fox."

"Your anger, Baby Bear, is useful when—action is required."

Baby Bear squeezed a familiar hand. "Again, you

are a rock in the turbulent currents of life. Has any of our business surrogates been contacted?"

"They have been queried online. Baby Raven is a whiz at tracking all internet activities around any of our affiliated businesses and foundations."

"So we must alert them that they will be visited by tomorrow."

"Our surrogates are ignorant of The Mission. They will give up little."

The two individuals embraced and kissed. "As long as we have each other, Baby Fox, our Mission will succeed."

Baby Bear crumpled up the newspaper and handed it to Baby Fox. "This will make a good fire starter."

9.

The FBI and Homeland Security arranged for additional aerial photographs and surveillance of the entire Olalla and related areas. However, the thickly forested communities reduced the effectiveness of such tactics. Thus, Kim and Audrey had to use old-school methods to pin down the ownership and boundaries of the land and structures in the areas of interest. They traveled to the Kitsap County Courthouse and Administration in Port Orchard, Washington.

County property records were open to the public, so subpoenas were unnecessary. The voluminous nature of the forms and documents of such an old-settled area was daunting. When the local clerks were told the reason for two federal agents searching the records, they jumped in to help. They accessed the computer database and tried to cross-reference it to many of the older paper records.

Thanks to the clerks' assistance, they discovered the plat maps for land owned by the World Education Group in one hour.

"Any office addresses?" asked Kim.

The clerk named Tracie shook her head 'no,' then continued. "However, I recognize this name here as a local attorney." Tracie pointed to a name on the deed form for a large tract of land.

"Hans Berg. He has an office in an old, refurbished house two blocks from the courthouse. Here, I'll show you on the Port Orchard city map."

"Do the records mention how long he has been the lawyer of record for the World Education Group?" Audrey asked.

"For this property, two years. Hans has practiced law in Port Orchard for some twenty years. Everyone knows him; he is a fixture at the Sons of Norway Hall."

Kim smiled at Audrey. "Well, shall we walk over and see Mister Berg?"

"Yes, Kim. I could use the exercise."

The former home and now office still had the original hardwood floors from prior decades. Hans was in his office eating some honest Danish (and Norwegian) pastries from a well-known bakery in downtown Poulsbo, Washington.

"Pardon my stuffing my face, but these goodies are habit-forming." Hans wiped crumbs from his beard as he spoke. "How can I help you, young ladies?"

"Well, sir," said Audrey, "you are handling a property for World Education Group."

"Yes. The Neilsen Twins approached me about two years ago to purchase a property from an estate. The deceased left no heirs, and the will mandated that the property be sold to a nonprofit and the purchase price donated to various organizations. I was the dead person's attorney and searched for a viable nonprofit. The Neilsens were the first to contact me, and their bonafide was in order. So, they bought the property and structures."

"They paid cash," Kim stated.

"Yes, they did. And I made all the necessary financial transaction reports as state and federal laws required. May I ask why the FBI and Homeland Security are interested? "

"A recently deceased sex offender was found on the rental property vacated by World Education Group."

"Hmm. I seem to remember something on the Internet about that death. However, I think the operative word is 'vacated' as the nonprofit had left. Thus, the death may have occurred after the Neilsens left the area."

"True," interjected Audrey, "and the Neilsens and their staff may have seen or heard something concerning the deceased. So, we would like to speak with them."

The attorney frowned. "I don't know about any staff," he said. "I only dealt with the Neilsens."

"How many times did you meet the Twins?" asked Kim.

"In person, just at the final signing. Sam and Sam are very private."

"Sam and Sam?"

"Samuel and Samantha are their legal names. They prefer to be gender non-specific. I don't think it has anything to do with sexual relationships; they want to be independent of any stereotypes."

"They like to be mysterious and private," said Audrey.

"I think you hit the nail on the head, Agent. Other than the final signing, all the other meetings were Zoom."

"Well, can you reach out to them?" asked Kim. "We need to talk with them. I hate to start banging on doors; it tends to cause people to clam up."

The Special Agents could have mentioned that law enforcement personnel were already roving around the area once Kim and Audrey obtained the address in Olalla. However, if the children were concealed on the property, the sudden appearance of law enforcement might result in a dangerous situation. Panic made people do stupid things.

Hans Berg showed signs of hesitation. The pastries had put him in a happy mood that was rapidly disappearing. The Suspicious Lawyer reared its head.

"They are not suspects, are they? I may not be their retained criminal lawyer, but I am still a lawyer."

"We are hoping they saw something," answered Audrey.

"Is this about the missing children?"

Kim smiled at Hans. "Well, the cat is out of the bag. The dead sex offender may have had contact with some of the children. We really hope the Neilsen Twins saw or heard something during their time in Tacoma."

The attorney was visibly relaxed. "Well, I know they are not in danger of being suspects."

"How so?" asked Audrey.

"Hell, they work with various churches and foster children groups. That is why I was so quick to deal with them. They have a reputation of helping with substantial funding and their time disadvantaged youth."

"Any reason why?"

"Go ahead and do some digging, Agents. They could be poster children for the horrors of child abuse in the adoption and foster care system. Their adopted name was Robins." Hans snorted. "Their so-called parents were rich in money but bankrupt in human emotion and caring."

"So, how did they wind up with World

Education Group?"

"The Robins died in a car crash; the minor children inherited everything and built it up from there. Their biological family, Neilsen, Sam, and Sam, the twins, contacted them and began using the millions to set up the foundations they use under the Neilsen name. Genius runs in the blood, despite the abuse they suffered from the Robins."

"So you would be willing to set up a meeting?" asked Kim.

"It may be a Zoom meeting, but yeah. Just as long as it is no attempt at an ambush."

"Perish the thought," Audrey replied, secretively winking at Kim.

The two Special Agents waited in the foyer of the law office as Hans Berg made a private telephone call to the Neilsen Twins.

"Think it was a mistake letting Hans in on the specifics?" asked Audrey.

"Hell, he'd find out eventually. This area is too small to keep a secret for long. Somebody will notice all the activity in Olalla, and more details on recovering Grette are about to hit the major news outlets."

"Well, I have a gut feeling that either these Twins are involved, or one of their organizations and staff are connected."

"Strangely, they disappeared from the Tacoma

location right when a pedophile was whacked."

"Yes, Kim. However, someone wiped that area so clean that connecting them for prosecution will be difficult."

"Well, maybe an interview will help. At least we will know precisely with whom we are dealing."

A few minutes later, Hans Berg contacted them in the foyer, shaking his head as he spoke. "I don't know why but Sam and Sam said they would come to my office and talk to you face to face. After all the resistance to personal contact over the past months, they agree to meet two complete strangers."

"Maybe they want to help," said Audrey. "After all, you said they have been involved in helping disadvantaged children for years."

"Hmmm. That's very true. Well, I guess we should not look a gift horse in the mouth, should we?"

"When did they say they could meet?"

"They'll be here in an hour and a half. They said they are at one of their subsidiaries outside Kitsap County. If you two would like to wait here—"

"Thanks, "replied Kim, "But we can grab some lunch and meet them back here."

"Alright. Then I will see you back here in about ninety minutes."

The Agents shook hands with the attorney and departed.

"So, you want to watch the Neilsens arrive?" asked Audrey.

"Yep. I want a make, model, and license plate of the vehicle they use and see if any other 'staff' drives them."

"You are as sneaky as I am, Kim."

"That's why we get along so well. Come on. I know the Sikh owner of the Seven Eleven down the hill on Bay Street. We can grab some sandwiches, and maybe he heard something about missing children."

It was like Old Home Week when the Stop and Rob owner saw Kim. "Namaste," they greeted each other with prayerful hands and slight bows.

"You must be working nearby to visit again," the owner Yashveer Singh, said in Punjabi.

"You have caught me," Kim said with a smile. *"I should stop by more often."*

"A famous member of the Punjab and Sikh community is always welcome to share her current exploits," the 7-11 owner said with a grin.

"Audrey, this is Yashveer Singh, a local business owner and friend of my father. "Kim said in English. "Audrey DiStefano is an FBI Agent out of Seattle."

As Yashveer shook Audrey's hand, he said, "This is about the missing children."

"You should have been an investigator instead of a businessman," replied Kim.

Yashveer shrugged. "You hear things in business, especially at a convenience stare down from the County Court House. Please feel free to ask the community for help. People who abduct children are the lowest of the low. However, you did find one, yes?"

"Yes, we did," Audrey replied. "Here is my card. Please feel free to contact us with even the vaguest of rumors. We still have other children to find."

"Let me make you some fresh coffee and tea. Sandwiches are on me," said Yashveer.

Fifteen minutes later, the two Special Agents had an eyeball on the attorney's office entrance door as they ate their lunches in the government vehicle.

"Kim, you made some contacts working those cases in Kitsap County."

"Yes, Audrey. A certain large feline kept me busy over here for a while."

"Well, let's hope they help in this case. At least we will get a look at these siblings of interest."

Kim sipped her tea and then replied, "I hope we get more than a look from this interview. I really want to know the Neilsen's answer about a certain body found in a former rental property."

"You and me both, my friend. You and me both."

"Are you sure this is a good idea?" Baby Fox asked. "Why agree to a face-to-face interview now?"

"If we don't, it will arouse more suspicion,"

replied Baby Bear. "We must present that World Education Group has nothing to hide." Baby Bear frowned.

"If only a few of our staff had not made grave errors that drew attention. And that piece of scum we had to eliminate."

"Someone must have tipped off the authorities in Tacoma," replied Baby Fox. "The body should not have been found for weeks.

"We dealt with that so far. There is nothing illegal about expanding an organization into different locations. We are connected with many other independent groups dealing with children, the foster parent situation, and still-existing orphanages. If contacted, every one of them will give WEG high marks and provide sterling reports about how we help children of all ages and backgrounds, including victims of human trafficking. The so-called money trail will show a non-profit started with extensive inheritance money."

Baby Fox hugged the Twin.

"We have spent millions on helping others. Plus, the Mission is righteous. God is on our side. I just know it."

Baby Bear returned the hug.

"When the world hears of what we have done and why they will rally to our cause. When we tell people our story about the horrors we suffered, they will be moved to act."

Baby Bear's hands formed into fists.

"If, after all that, the sheep refuse to look up and resist the One World Government and the harm it is doing to children—they will reap the whirlwind."

"There they are," said Kim. The special agents obtained some driver's licenses and business license photos of the listed officers of the WEG when the Tacoma property landlord had first identified those involved.

"They do look a lot alike," said Audrey. "Both around five-eight in height, short cut light brown hair, medium complexion. Wearing those matching jumpsuits makes it hard to tell their biological gender."

"Do you think they are truly transgender or just androgynous?"

"I think they dislike being classified by society. I still get irritated when people try to decide if I am straight or lesbian rather than treat me as an individual."

"That would make sense, based on their experience with the foster system. I imagine they dealt with much bureaucratic pigeonholing before and after they were turned over to the Robins."

"That is a nice dark blue SUV," said Kim as she went old school and used a 35MM camera with a telephoto lens to click a series of photographs. Audrey texted the vehicle license plate to Homeland Security Sector Communications to obtain a quick response.

"Of course, the plates registration return to

World Education Group," said the FBI agent.

"It makes sense that they will keep everything registered to the primary nonprofit. Fewer headaches from the IRS and state departments of revenue and licensing."

"I was hoping they would give us another lead to check out. No such luck."

"Well, Audrey, let me secure this camera in the trunk. Then, we interrupt any long-winded briefing our lawyer friend will try to give these persons of interest."

The Neilsen Twins were just shown into Hans Berg's office when the two agents brushed by the receptionist before the lawyer could shut his door.

"Hi, there!" called out Audrey. "Glad you could make it for a short conversation."

"Now Agents—" Berg said, interrupted by one of the Twins.

"We are glad to be here. We fear misinformation is impacting our reputation and the World Education Group."

"I am Special Agent Audrey DiStefano, FBI. And my friend here is Special Agent Kim Kupar from Homeland Security."

"May we introduce ourselves? I am Sam Neilsen, as is my twin, Sam Neilsen. To preclude confusion, I can be called Samuel and my sister Samantha." He smiled as he continued. "Your first question will be why we use the same name and do not usually differentiate by gender."

"Actually," interjected Kim, "no, that is not our first question. Rather, we need to talk about the property you leased in Tacoma and recently left."

"Straight and to the point," Samantha said. "We appreciate that attitude. We have many so-called irons in the fire about the mission of the World Education Group and don't have time to waste."

"You're here to ask about a dead body found after we moved out of the Tacoma address," said Samuel.

Kim noticed the two fraternal twins looked so similar that she had trouble telling them apart. The federal investigator thought Samuel's Adams Apple was a bit more pronounced. However, dressed identically and of the same body size and height, picking them out at a distance would be extremely difficult. Kim concentrated on Samuel's statement and away from the appearance.

"I take it you have contacted your former landlord."

"He telephoned us quite agitated," said Samantha. "He seemed as upset that we soundproofed parts of the building as he was about the corpse."

"You realize how it would seem suspicious that you left, and then a body was discovered. And then there was the door boarded over."

"The door we simply secured, not boarded it

over," said the brother. "And to jump to the chase, as it were, we left because an unsavory element became more prevalent in the neighborhood. You Agents must know that we sometimes had children visitors at our locations. Helping and nurturing disadvantaged, orphaned, and foster children are the primary mission of WEG."

"So, did you know the deceased?" asked Audrey.

"We would need a photograph to say for sure. Do you have one?"

Kim presented an Identification photo from Community Corrections. The Twins examined the picture and shook their heads in unison.

"No, he's not familiar," said Samantha.

"He does not have a pleasant face," added Samuel.

"He was a convicted pedophile," said Audrey.

"His Karma caught up with him," said Samantha.

"We would never let anyone of that ilk anywhere near our children," Samuel said. "We work with non-profits and government organizations, including the Polaris Project, to combat such abuse. Hans Beck here can provide many details of our activities due to the requirements of interacting with orphaned and foster children."

"Our reputation among the various related organizations is beyond reproach," added Samantha. "We will provide you with a list of all the groups and organizations we worked with over the years."

"We will appreciate that," said the FBI agent. "Somehow, among all the child pornography and trafficking investigations, your organization's name did not come up."

"We strive to stay in the background," replied Samuel. "Publicity and media attention distracts from the mission of WEG."

"Which is?" Interjected Kim.

"To prevent the abuse we endured from so-called loving foster parents," said Samuel. "Government bureaucracy should not stand in the way of children receiving the love and care they need after being separated from their biological family."

"That happened to you also. You were removed from your biological mother's home."

"Yes. Our mother was placed in a mental institution after our father disappeared. Our biological relatives were deemed unfit to raise us for some reason."

Kim noticed Samuel's jaw was tight, and his carotid artery seemed pronounced. A subject that pushed the Twins' buttons was evident.

His sibling also noticed as she placed a calming hand on Sam's arm.

"We take this subject seriously and personally," Samantha said. "Our experience growing up was far from pleasant."

"I am sorry to hear that," replied Kim. "I know if

someone abused my children—well, there would be Hell to pay."

"You are the Tiger Lady involved with a unique child trafficking investigation in Port Angeles," said Samantha.

"You could say that, but we have twelve missing Children of Color this day."

"But, of course," answered Samuel. "Accept my apology if my reactions distracted us from the subject at hand."

"Could we visit your local property and see your efforts in the flesh?" interjected Audrey.

The Twins paused and glanced at each other.

"If you want to see how we treat children," said Samantha, "you must wait a few days. Our field trips and other activities have been suspended for a few days as we become used to the location near Olalla."

"So, you have no children staying with you?"

"Not this moment."

"The children a State Trooper saw you with— where are they?"

"Back with their families or other support groups," Samuel replied. "We only keep children under our care for extended times when no other options exist. Please give us your contact information, and we promise we'll contact you once we are settled in the current location. The move from the Tacoma location was rushed."

"How about we arrange a visit forty-eight hours from now?" asked Audrey. "We need to proceed with this investigation promptly."

"So we are suspects," replied Samantha.

"Persons of interest or possible witnesses," replied Kim. "Since a missing child was recovered in your area, we are checking all the residences and property in and near Olalla. Yours is one of many."

The Twins paused for a minute, then spoke in unison. "Fine. Forty-Eight hours."

"May we have your business cards?" asked Samuel.

"Of course."

After exchanging business cards (WEG had their own), the Neilsens each slightly bowed and said their goodbyes.

"You act as if they are under suspicion," grumbled Hans Berg. "You'll apologize once you discover they're well respected in the foster and orphan children community. And that does not even mention their work with child sex trafficking victims."

"Well, Mister Berg," replied Kim. "My apologizing won't be the first time nor the last."

The Agents left the law office in time to see the Neilsens drive off in the dark-colored SUV.

"Waddaya think?" asked Audrey.

"I think they are hiding something," answered Kim. "The question is whether it concerns the remaining missing Children of Color."

"Well, let's run them through our various databases and see if World Education Group is actually that well respected and active."

"Good idea, But first, let me treat you to some of the best Texas Barbecue in Western Washington."

"Where is that, Kim?"

"*BBQ2U* in Gig Harbor. I bet it is the best barbeque you'll eat, better than any you had in Texas."

"You're on."

"Are they suspicious of us?" asked Samantha in the SUV.

"Of course, they are, my sibling. That is why they wanted to question us."

"They will now attempt a search warrant based on their suspicions."

"Which will be difficult, based on our public record." Samuel patted his sibling's leg. "They will visit us in a few days without a search warrant. The agents will hope they see something they can use to obtain a warrant."

"So, we must prevent that, Samuel."

"Oh, we will prevent them from some enforcement action," replied Samuel with a grin. "For we will use them as a—captive audience to the announcement of our Mission."

"You wish to let the world know, now? I did not think we were ready."

"Grette escaping has forced our hand. But unlike Koresh at Waco, we will be in control of the time and place of our declaration. The world will be forced to look in the mirror and realize how corrupt they are when it comes to the safety of children."

Samantha took Samuel's hand.

"As long as we have each other, we will overcome any obstacle, any evil. Just like we overcame our so-called adopted parents."

Samuel squeezed her hand.

"That was such an efficient action on your part, Samantha. It allowed all of… *this* to occur."

"It was God's Will, Samuel. It was God's Will."

Audrey pushed herself back from the *BBQ2U* table.

"I think I am royally stuffed, Kim. This meal will require many hours of work in the Dojo to allow me to fit into my clothes."

"Now admit it, Audrey. This meal is better than any barbecue you had."

"I stand in awe of your selection and knowledge of Western Barbecue for one steeped in Eastern knowledge."

Kim laughed and then replied. "You keep forgetting my family connection with Argentine beef through my mother. She is a connoisseur of good meat."

"I bow to your mother's expertise. And I plan on a return trip here."

"Gary Parker, the owner, appreciates return customers. He also enjoys local authors and writers, so he has them signing books in the Book Nook at the front."

"You should write a book, Kim. You have a unique perspective and interesting experiences."

"Which means I could never receive permission to write such a book. Some of the investigations are still restrictive access."

"Well, things change. Maybe when your twins are older."

"Don't wish their lives away yet, Audrey. Give me a chance to enjoy them while they are still young." Kim looked at the time on her cellphone.

"Let's head back to our offices and get out intelligence analysts working on WEG and the Neillsens. Hopefully, they can turn something new while I spend time with my husband and children."

10.

A day later, the intelligence analysts found information that supported Hans Berg's assessment. The Neilsens and WEG were well respected among the human trafficking and child sexual abuse investigative community. The Polaris Project and the National Center for Missing & Exploited Children gave glowing reports on the activities of the World Education Group. The Neilsens provided funding, education, and media attention to the entire gamut of child abuse and sex trafficking.

"Any negative or questionable information at all?" asked Kim.

"Just that their parents died of a car crash involving brake failure," Audrey replied. "Plus, articles talk about just how the Twins suffered under the control of the Robins, And 'control' is the operative word. The adoptive parents dressed them alike and marched them around like automatons. The Robins liked to use them to display how woke and progressive they were in adopting two abandoned twins."

"Abandoned?"

"Their biological parents, the Neilsens, had severe substance abuse problems. The mother wound up in a mental institution, and the father disappeared. Child Protective Services found the Twins in a filthy motel room at age two. They were next placed in the foster care network, and the Robins showed up. Money talks, so the adoption was expedited, maybe illegally, or at least against regulations."

"The parents died at age thirteen," said Kim.

"Yep. An uncle jumped in as a guardian as part of the will. He helped manage the wealth until they reached the age of majority, eighteen. The Twins took over and soon began expanding the already substantial wealth."

"So they had a natural ability at finance, it seems."

"Uncle John also died within a year of the Twins receiving access to the financial mini-empire. Uncle John was unmarried and left his estate to the Twins. A year later, World Education Group began building a full empire."

"Any idea how much they are worth?"

"Being a nonprofit, WEG has millions of non-taxable funds. The Twins are still millionaires in their own right. They are pretty anal about keeping a wall between the nonprofit and their personal wealth, even though all their work is within the nonprofit."

"So they are the example of rich paragons of virtue," said Kim. "Yet, two dead bodies have turned up in this investigation; one connected to a property they occupied."

"So, what is the next step, Kim? I doubt we have enough for a search warrant because of their history as paragons of virtue. I bet most of the judges in the area know their reputation of fighting child exploitation and abuse."

"Yes, I agree. The dead sex offender will not add any credence to our suspicions. What is one more dead pedophile in the greater scheme of things?"

"So…"

"So, Audrey, we pay them a visit and snoop for more probable cause to support a warrant. They invited us to see their local residence. They believe we will be less suspicious by being open and straightforward."

"That attitude makes me more suspicious. It is almost like they want us to find something so they can explain it away."

"I think they have a high level of hubris. After all, the rest of us are mere mortals."

"Why don't you head home, Kim? Spend some time with your family while I set up the visit."

"You don't have to break my arm, Audrey. See you tomorrow."

"Have fun for me also. You can come back and give me all the details. I need to live vicariously."

Hank met her at the door, holding the twins. Kim smiled and set her briefcase down, and reached for her children. She took the twins in her arms as they smiled and made gurgling noises.

"They miss you—as I do," Hank said.

"Well, my love, we have reached a point in the investigation where we will have a definite conclusion or be off in a different direction. Either may lead to an end of late nights soon."

"You have a target?"

"We seem to have targets. However, they are so strange that pinning them down may be an issue, leading the agencies involved to step back and reassess. That always slows things down."

"Well, whatever happens. Be careful. And do not worry about the twins. I will ensure they are healthy, wealthy, and wise."

Kim leaned forward and kissed her husband. "I know you will, dearest. I know you will."

"Come on, Kim. I'll make you dinner while you feed the twins. They prefer your breasts over bottles."

Two mornings later, Kim and Audrey drove to the Olalla property of the World Education Group. As they prepared earlier, Audrey had said, "Wear your undercover body armor, Kim."

"You have a feeling about this?"

"Yes, Kim. My Spidey Combat Sense is tingling up a storm. You know Olalla was the site of Starvation Heights."

"So you think the Neilsens may be rich quacks?"

"Or worse."

"I will never question the gut feeling of a combat Marine. So. On goes the body armor."

Discussions with the two agencies' supervisors resulted in Tim Weiss occupying an office at the State Patrol substation near Auto Dealer Row on the south end of Bremerton. From there, he could monitor communications and ensure a timely response if the interview with the Neilsens went bad.

"If anything looks off—" said Weiss.

"We back off and yell for help," interjected Kim.

"Agent Deistefano, I expect you to help keep Kim here from going off half-cocked. At times she is much too aggressive for her own good."

"Yes, Sir," answered Audrey as she suppressed a smile. "I'll ensure she gets home to her twins."

"Good. Glad we are all on the same wavelength. Do a radio check before you enter the property. And again, be careful."

Kim drove the Mustang G-ride to a new-looking iron gate an hour later. She pressed the call button on the pole-attached intercom next to the entrance.

"Can I help you?" asked a female voice.

"Agents Kupar and DiStefano here to talk to

the Neilsens."

There was a buzzing sound, and the iron gate swung open. "Please enter. Follow the painted arrows to the vehicle parking area."

"Here goes," said Audrey just before she keyed the vehicle radio microphone. After the check-in, the two Agents had an hour to call in for another security check. Failure to do so would have Tim Weiss sending someone to check, then the calvary if necessary.

The entire property was heavily wooded, the Neilsens keeping the original old-growth trees and brush.

"No wonder our drones and aircraft couldn't identify much," said Kim. "This reminds me of the Olympic National Forest."

"Hopefully, there are no lions, tigers, and bears around," said Audrey.

"Sir Khan would help out here, Audrey."

The parking area sat in front of a multi-storied structure that resembled more of a good-sized resort than a residence.

"Looks like most of this is new construction. Just the center portion looks like an original entrance to a farmhouse."

"Hmmm. Kim, I don't remember seeing a lot of new building permits at the County offices."

"It was done off the books during the lockdowns. That, Audrey, may give us an in to make them uncomfortable."

Kim parked the car in a Visitors spot as the two agents sought a welcoming committee.

"I guess they trust us to find the correct entry door," said Audrey.

"We are on Candid Camera. They are watching our every move, Audrey."

"Well, shall we exit the car and give them some laughs as we stumble about?"

Kim laughed. "Hell, why not."

The two women walked towards the older-looking double doors on an equally old portion of the front porch. The boards of the steps and porch creaked and complained as Kim and Audrey walked up to the entrance. Just as Kim was about to knock, Samantha Neilsen opened the door.

"Welcome to our home and workplace," the Twin said with a smile. Kim noticed the sometimes-identified female wearing a light blue jumpsuit and matching running shoes.

"We are glad you allowed us to visit you here," replied Audrey. "You spent some time and effort in modernization."

"Yes, we did. This campus often houses the less fortunate from the foster and orphanage systems."

"You kept much of the original porch and front steps," added Kim.

"The squeaks and groans of the old wood remind us how old and crotchety the Washington State Child

Protective Service is," answered Samantha.

"As well as tell you when you have visitors."

"Yes again, Agent Kupar."

Samantha stepped back and motioned with a sweep of her arm for the two Agents to enter.

"We have a short briefing for you in the front room. Then we will take you on the proverbial grand tour."

Despite their apparent age, the rugs on the original hardwood floors were lush and well-kept. They entered a large former dining room and saw Samuel standing near a small table with a large computer screen setting on it.

"We are so glad you came, Kim and Audrey," Samuel said, ending the greeting with a large grin. "You will be special conduits for presenting our mission to the world."

"We're just here to discover new leads for recovering the missing children," interjected Audrey. "Your foundation's mission is not our area of interest-." Audrey stopped speaking as six large men and two women stepped out from curtain-covered alcoves. The FBI Agent moved her hand to her pistol as the Agents saw all eight adults wearing animal-imaged detailed masks.

"What is with the welcoming committee?" asked Kim as she turned to face the opposite side of the room.

"It is time, my friends," said Samuel. The eight masked adults rushed the Agents in unison.

John Richards drove the SUV for another trip of trading fruit for eggs. With prices rising, swapping an overabundance of fruit from their orchards at Orchard House was an excellent cost-cutting tactic.

"You kids are way too quiet back there," said his raven-haired wife, Rebecca. "Are you slipping apples to Snow and Blackie again?"

"We have plenty," said the fraternal twins Jack and Jill in unison.

Rebecca sighed. The twins had inherited equal amounts of Muleness from each parent. She turned in the front passenger seat and saw the two massive dogs grinning in their canine fashion as they sat in the third seat area in the ultimate back of the SUV. With smiles like that, she could not be angry.

"Okay. Keep it up, and no eggs for cakes and breakfast."

"Mom—"

Further conversation was interrupted as both dogs growled in unison. Rebecca noticed they were both staring out the driver's side windows.

"What's up?" asked John.

"I don't know—wait. We are not far from where we found Grette on the road."

"Bad memories, Rebecca?"

"No. We know our canines are special and very sensitive. Pull over for a moment."

The retired ParaRescueman drove the SUV onto the right shoulder of the Kitsap County Road. Rebecca unbuckled her seat belt and exited the passenger side.

"Stay in the car, twins," she said in her best Mom Voice. Rebecca stepped to the rear of the vehicle and opened the hatchback. A second later, the two large K-9s almost bowled her over as they shot from the SUV.

"Son of a bitch," said John as he turned the SUV engine off and clambered from the driver's seat.

"Language," said the twins.

"Blackie! Snow!" Rebecca called out as the dogmates dashed across the road and into the forest.

John pulled his ten-millimeter Glock pistol from his holster as he watched the two dogs disappear like spirits of the woods.

"Rebecca, you stay with the kids. Those two beasts would not ignore you unless something terrible were happening."

"Why do you get to have fun?" asked his wife.

"Because I am the USAF-trained killer."

"I thought you were into rescue?"

"Sometimes that requires extreme violence. Like when I saved you from some nasty Afghanis."

Rebecca quickly hugged and kissed her husband. "You be careful, Stud."

"I will. Remember, I have what seems to be two

Pookas in the shape of dogs to protect me."

"Hurry back. I'll sit on this road so you can find us."

"Roger that." John then jogged into the brush where the dogs had disappeared.

Rebecca went to the driver's seat and started the SUV. "Keep an eye out for Dad and the dogs, kids."

"Will they be okay?" asked Jack.

"Yep. Three of the orneriest creatures on this side of Puget Sound are on a mission. Woe to those who interfere."

11.

Kim tested her restraints for the umpteenth time while listening to Audrey spit blood. The FBI Agent took the brunt of the violence after she shot one of the men in the foot. The minion was still cursing up a storm as the one called Baby Rabbit saw to his injury.

Kim had planted a strong kick into the solar plexus of one of the masked miscreants before she was restrained by sheer body weight. Her primary and backup pistols were now in the Neilsens' followers' hands, as was her and Audrey's body armor. The attack was so unexpected, yet she still kicked herself for not being more cautious. Now the two Agents resided in a basement room of recent construction.

"You know if we do not check-in, other agents will come," Kim said to Samantha.

"The more, the better audience," replied the Twin, now sporting a Baby Fox mask. "However, we have arranged a delay in noticing you are missing. You forced us to move up our Mission. It will still be completed."

"And what mission is that?" said Audrey, her mouth temporarily free of bloody saliva. "Some mad ranting about the Zionist Occupation Government?"

Samuel smiled at her as he spoke. "Of course, you have us classified as insane conspiracy theorists, Agent. How little you know of what we have seen and experienced."

"Well, enlighten us, Sam. Please explain why you kidnap young children and terrify their parents. Justify keeping the children under lock and key, drugged with happy juice."

Samuel grinned as he answered. "Ignorant people like yourself prove why we must take the children to save them. You must have found in your searches of our backgrounds what my sibling and I suffered at the hands of the State managed foster and adoption system. Yet, people in various organizations and the media play a lip surface in improving a broken system. How tiring it is to hear "we care" and see the continually abused 'products,' the children paraded about as if they were not damaged."

"So you seize two federal agents to make an even bigger statement," interjected Kim. "You will have a short 'media frenzy' at your behest; then you will spend years in prison."

"You think we were not already in prison as children?" asked Samantha. "From horrible foster homes to adoption by alleged loving parents, we were used and abused. And who cared? No One!"

The female sibling advanced on the restrained agents.

"You think we are crazy monsters. Yet, you know the children we have are happy and healthy."

"Oh yeah?" Audrey spat out. "Ask Grette how she felt. Ask her why she fled to find her mother. The children seem happy because you drugged them."

"You misunderstand the necessity of taking the children to save them and others," Samuel broke in. "Despite years of pleading and preaching by various officials and organizations, millions of children are used and abused by us adults every year. Both biological and adopted parents prey on the weakest humans; the children."

"Which happened with your biological family, yes?" said Kim. "So now you kidnap children like you were and scare them to save them."

"The fear is only temporary. The children soon feel our love and enjoy the world we created."

"Oh, yeah. Love from people wearing these funky animal masks," Audrey spat out. "You realize COVID showed the need for children to see human faces to achieve sufficient socialization. Humans read each other as individuals through facial expressions—"

"Quit trying to lecture us," interrupted Samantha. "You act as if we have not spent years studying the problems of child-rearing and child abuse. And again, you ignore our personal journey through abuse. You don't think that gives us a unique ability to deal with the problem in society?"

"I think you are too close to the problem. Sometimes you need to step back and examine your actions. "

"Actions? We are saving children from abuse. Our actions will shock the system and society so much that people will be forced to change!"

Kim saw Samantha's eyes take on the visage of a fanatic.

"Audrey, I think they have made up their minds," said the new mother of twins. "They have justified their illegal actions in their minds and must suffer the consequences."

"Yes, we will suffer for the Mission," added Samuel. "Many great people throughout history martyred themselves to achieve a good."

"You must destroy the village to save it," said Audrey.

"Pardon me?" asked Samuel with a frown.

"In Viet Nam, a young officer told a news crew they had to burn down a village to keep it from falling into Communist hands."

"This is not Viet Nam."

"Yeah, but it looks a lot like Waco. My agency wound up killing over twenty children to supposedly save them. This standoff you plan has all the markings of providing a dozen child-sized coffins."

The Neilsen Twins' faces flushed with rage. Samuel strode over to Audrey and then Kim, slapping each hard.

"How dare you suppose our actions will seriously harm the children! Any harm will be caused by the heavy hand of the government, not the World Education Group and its love."

"You set the ball rolling, Samuel," said Kim. "Sometimes, like falling rocks, an uncontrolled landslide will result. You have time to stop it and still get your points across."

"You just want to talk your way out," replied Samantha. "It is too late for a new path. The die is cast. The children will survive." The sibling glared at the Agents. "I think you may not."

John Richards tried to catch up with the two oversized canines in the thick Northwest Washington brush. The canines seemed to thread their way through the forest rather than loudly crashing and creating a pathway. John tried to follow their lead as best he could as he stumbled through the thick woods. He did not want to smack into someone or something he needed to avoid.

John thought he glimpsed the white fur of Snow through the trees and headed in that direction. The dogs were not barking; they were acting like a hunting wolfpack sneaking up on prey. That thought gave John pause as he checked the condition of his Glock pistol. When he left the military, he thought he had left all such stress and danger behind.

"Fat chance," John mumbled.

He heard a loud male voice yell. "Dog, get back. Shoo. Go away!"

A single bark let John pinpoint the dogs. He hurried forward and then yelled. "Hey, Buddy! I am just trying to get my dogs. They went after a squirrel or something."

"Get them and leave," said the voice. "You are coming on private property. Here, we can shoot stray dogs threatening livestock in rural farmland."

"Hey, cool it," replied John. He moved forward and discovered he could now see a large man through a break in the vegetation. The figure wore a Halloween-style mask of some animal and carried a semiauto rifle.

"Snow, Blackie, come here. You do not want to be shot."

The two dogs suddenly came bounding through the woods to where John stood. Then, they were past him and running into another section of the forest.

"Leave and don't come back," ordered the masked figure. "This area is private property and posted no trespassing."

"Sorry. The dogs must have missed the signs. We are leaving."

John turned and tried to follow the canines. He dialed his cell phone as he created distance between himself and the sentry.

"Rebecca, can you call the contact number Kim and Audrey gave you? I think the dogs found someone who doesn't want to be found."

ASAC Tim Weiss was sipping his coffee and checked his watch once more. The hour check-in for the Agents was due. Then a State Trooper stuck his head into the office where Sam was camped out.

"Line three, Sir."

"Thanks."

"ASAC Weiss here. Hello, Rebecca. How are— What? Where? You tell John to stay put and out of the way. I'll send someone to check things out. Kupar and DiStefano are in the area."

The ASAC ended the call and called on the Radio. "Alpha 312, this is Alpha 201. Any contact with the Agents on the interview?"

Sam had an "eyeball" unit on the gated driveway entrance to the WEG property.

"Alpha 312 here. The two Agents just left the area."

"You saw them driving away?"

"Yes sir, Two females in the G-ride with the tinted windows."

"Okay. Affirmative, Thanks."

Tim tried the cellphones of both Agents and received the 'person you have called is unavailable right now' message. He cursed as he knew coverage was intermittent in the Olalla area. Radio calls to Kim were unanswered.

The ASAC sat and pondered for a moment, then cursed some more. Could the Neilsens be so psychotic that they would take Kim's G-ride and make it appear they left the property?

After five more minutes, and if there was no contact, it was time to send a standby unit to the entrance gate and achieve communication.

"I never should have let those two go in. This situation is looking like all one big setup!"

"John, the supervisors say to lay low; units are responding."

"Yeah, right, Rebecca. They are not going to be able to get anywhere near the residence. The assholes are waiting for them."

"And what is a non-law enforcement person going to do? You are not a PJ and not on active duty."

"Once a PJ, always a PJ. And I am not about to let our dogs get shot."

"Dammit, John. This situation is not your fight."

"Tell that to Snow and Blackie. They would disagree."

"John, they are dogs; we are the human masters."

"Yeah, right. Gotta go."

"John Richards, you stubborn ass!"

"They think the Agents left," reported Baby Gorilla. "Baby Raven just heard it on the radio."

"So much for encoded secure transmissions," said Audrey.

Samuel laughed. "You realize money and appearance of goodwill can open doors," the sibling replied. "Every code can be broken given enough time, effort, and money."

"So you may be getting the response you wished," interjected Kim. "The problem is will it have the desired effect?"

"It does not matter the results here," replied Samantha. "It matters the response in the world. The One World Government will be shaken to its core as we transmit our Mission Statement to all to see and hear."

"You think the U.S. government will allow that? Do you believe all the federal and state law enforcement agencies will not stop you from broadcasting anything to the media?"

"You forgot all the subsidiary groups and organizations affiliated with World Education Group. A few codes to some mainframes and specific computers, and viola! Our words spread beyond the confines of Washington State."

"Which does what?" Audrey spat out. "Shows

your crazy ass ideas for all to see? You kidnap innocent kids to prove a point? Yeah, that's really intelligent!"

"You have a nasty mouth," said Baby Gorilla. "Do you want her mouth shut, Baby Fox?"

"She is just trying to irritate and incite. Pay her no mind, Baby Gorrilla."

"Hey, Kim. This is the fool that Snow bit the crap out of when Grette escaped. Hey, Gorilla-face. Did you like a dog chewing on you when you tried to beat on a little girl? Big man, I see. Big, stupid, and smells like an ape in the monkey house at the zoo."

Baby Gorilla moved quickly for such a large man. An open hand slap knocked Audrey and her chair over.

"Baby Gorilla!" Samuel called out. "That is enough."

Audrey once again spat out blood. "You hit like a little bitch, ape face."

The masked man bellowed, picked up Audrey, chair and all, and threw her across the room. Samuel strode over and slapped Baby Gorilla's face, knocking his mask askew.

"*Stop it!*" Commanded Baby Bear. "You will follow orders or be told to leave the premises. Do you understand?"

Kim watched as the large man opened and closed his hands as if any second he would grab and break something- people or furniture. Finally, he replied. "Yes, Baby Bear. I hear and obey."

Samuel/Baby Bear glared at Kim as he spoke. "I suggest you convince your so-called partner to control her comments. Making Baby Gorilla and others angry will only result in unpleasant consequences."

"Your actions set the stage, Samuel Neilsen," answered Kim as she tested her bindings again. "Any violence is the result of your so-called Mission, nothing else. Now, can someone please help Audrey off the floor?"

A woman called Baby Ferret, wearing a mask matching her name, righted Audrey in her chair, which seemed partially broken apart. The FBI Agent spat blood on the floor once again.

"Slapping me around just shows your questionable morals and mental processes," said Audrey. "You refuse to admit to your failings. Victim, Victimizer, Victim. You are in the psychological cycle of many an abusive existence."

"You claim we are the abusers?" said Samuel. "Our actions will save thousands to millions from child abuse and sexual predation." The person known as Baby Bear had no mask to hide his raged, flushed face.

"You have no idea the abuse Samantha and I suffered at the hands of alleged loving adults. There are even pornographic photos we have tried to excise from the internet. Yet you claim *we* are victimizers?"

"As Audrey said," interjected Kim, "you're too close to the subject. You cannot see the cycle you and your helpers are locked in."

"We will see your attitude when your children are involved," said Samantha.

Kim glared at the Neilsen Twins. "I highly suggest you leave my children out of this."

"It may be too late for that, Kim Kupar. You reap what you sow."

Kim growled and tried to break her bounds once more.

12.

The front doorbell rang as Hank was placing the twins in their strollers. He thought walking around the neighborhood would help calm them and him down. They had not seen enough of their Mother and were fussy. Plus, Hank was worried. He knew Kim and Audrey were off interviewing some significant persons of interest. Times like these made Hank wish he could convince Kim it was time to look for another line of work.

"I'm coming," Hank called out as he finished strapping the twins in their strollers. He did not expect any deliveries. He hoped they weren't Mormons or Jehovah's Witnesses. Hank disliked being rude to young people, just doing what their religion asked of them.

Hank opened the door to a more petite figure in a

blue set of coveralls wearing an M-95 mask.

"Can I help you?" asked Hank.

"We have a delivery for a Kim Kupar at this address," replied the muffled feminine voice. Hank noticed two larger and similarly attired figures holding a six-foot-long box standing behind the first person.

"I don't know of any scheduled delivery. Can you double-check the paperwork?"

The female person before Hank shuffled papers as the two other delivery persons set the large box down.

"Let me see," the masked person said. Then one of the box carriers shot Hank with a Taser. The prongs of the cartridge stuck into Hank's neck as the shooter activated the electric charge. The father of the twins shook, stiffened, then toppled over.

"Grab the children," said the female. Seeing their father fall, the twins began to cry and howl in fear.

"Hurry, we need to calm the children—"

"Candygram."

A voice behind the three coverall-wearing persons caused them to all turn and look.

"I said Candygram, assholes," growled Rex Moyer as he laid his walking cane alongside the head of the Taser-wielding miscreant. The force of the blow not only laid the man out but also broke the walking stick. The remaining sharp point allowed the Retired Special Agent to stab the second male in the throat. As blood spurted from the neck wound, the female dropped the clipboard and reached inside a coverall pocket.

"*Don't!*" commanded T-Rex as a compact Star PD .45 pistol appeared in his hand. The masked figure yanked a snub nose revolver from a pocket and pointed it at the Retired Agent when her head exploded like a burst melon. The body collapsed to the ground.

"Goddamn fool. Now you're dead."

Hank moaned and tried to sit up, the Taser no longer shocking him with 50,000 volts.

"Stay down, Big Man. I've got you covered."

Rex Moyer moved to the twins while covering the three downed miscreants.

Hank lurched upright as the twins reached for their father from their strollers.

"Dad's here, Kids. Come on, no more crying." Hank looked at Rex as the older man moved to cover the kidnappers with his pistol while dialing 9-1-1 on his cell phone.

"Why are you here, Rex?" asked Hank.

"Thought I'd stop by and spoil the Munchkins. All mine are done grown and left."

"Thank God you did, T-Rex."

"Yeah. The Big Man Upstairs was watching out for us this day. Damn. Now I have to explain what happened—hello, Dispatch. This is Retired Federal Agent Rex Moyer. I need an aid car and backup. There has been an attempted kidnapping and shooting at the following address —"

"Say that again?" Tim Weiss growled over the telephone. "Some people just tried to kidnap Kim Kupar's children? Alright, activate the WET team we had on standby. I'll call the FBI supervisor to activate the standby HRT."

The ASAC set the phone down and keyed his radio. "Alpha-312, are you at the entrance gate?"

"Yes, Sir. No one will answer the intercom.—Wait a minute, someone is walking towards us. *Gun.*" The radio transmission ended.

"Fuck. All units on this channel. Officers need assistance, shots fired. Respond to the following location—"

"Your twins will be under our control shortly," said Samuel. "The recovery team I sent is on site."

Kim glared at the fanatic. "What right do you have to take my children?" She growled.

"The right of a greater good. Society must change. Your children will be another catalyst—"

Kim let out a Banshee scream and jerked at her restraints. Cracking sounds emanated from the wooden chair where she sat tied.

"Baby Gorilla, check Kim Kupar's restraints. We will move her if necessary."

Audrey's damaged chair, set upright after Baby Gorilla's tantrum, creaked as Audrey twisted in her seat. The minions and their leaders looked at Kim in distraction. The FBI Agent felt a rope shift as she heard more wood cracking. Audrey managed to rise on her toes and then throw her weight backward. Her chair toppled over, and Audrey's right leg restraint broke loose.

Samuel yelled commands to the staff still in the room. Two helpers righted Audreys's chair as Baby Gorilla checked Kim's restraints. The huge man mumbled, then screamed in pain as Kim sank her teeth into his too-close face. A meaty hand clamped around Kim's jaw and squeezed, forcing Kim to release her bite. The HSI Agent spit the man's flesh and blood at him as Baby Gorilla stumbled back, cursing in pain.

"That is enough!" Samantha said. "Take these to the dark Time Out Closet. Let them wonder about their fate in darkness."

In a rage, Baby Gorilla lifted Kim over his head, chair and all. Before anyone could stop him, Kim was slammed down onto the cement floor. The Agent lay still in the broken wooden chair.

"Now, see what you have done! Get a new chair and some duct tape. We can tape her up like a mummy."

The FBI Hostage Rescue Team MRAP armored vehicle rolled up to the metal entrance gate to the World Education Group compound. Following in trail were two Homeland Security Warrant Entry Team SUVs transporting ten team members. The dozen FBI HRT agents added to the WET personnel meant twenty-two body armor and automatic weapon-equipped highly trained law enforcement officers responded to assist Kim and Audrey. Alpha-312 Special Agents had reversed their bullet-ridden vehicle into a ditch to find cover.

ASAC Weiss could not contact Kim and Audrey by radio or telephone. Thus, the teams were ordered in. The leader of the HRT used a loudspeaker to announce and demand entry.

"Federal Agents with warrants and exigent circumstances demand entry, Open the gate!"

The commands were met with silence. The FBI Senior Agent broadcast the demands twice more with equal nonresponse.

"Driver, ram the gate."

The former military vehicle slammed into the wrought iron gate and flattened it. The MRAP (Mine Resistant Ambush Protected) vehicle ran over the gate and proceeded 25 yards toward the primary residence. The MRAP crashed to a stop when automatic thick pillar bollards shot up out of the driveway, suspending the vehicle's front end.

"Shit," said the team leader as the driver failed to free the vehicle. "Alright, everyone, deploy tactically. We get to go for a jog."

The HSI WET team, seeing the surrounding brush and trees were too thick for the SUVs, followed the HRT in deploying on foot. Twenty-two law enforcement officers hurried up to the main buildings. Just moments after being forced from the tactical vehicles, hydraulic-launched metal spears crisscrossed the asphalt driveway. Each spear dragged an attached metal cable across the entrance trail. One HRT Agent who moved faster than the rest caught a pike across his legs. All the officers went to the dirt to dodge all the flying metal.

"Team members are down. Team members are down," the FBI Senior Agent broadcasts over the radio net.

"How in the Hell did they get building permits *for this?*" Someone called out.

"They didn't ask," the Senior Agent responded. "They just did it."

"The rescuers are stopped," reported the minion known as Baby Raven.

"They will keep coming," said Audrey.

"We are broadcasting our message as we speak," replied Samantha. "The media and the world know we have two federal agents as hostages, not to mention the twelve children."

"So you admit the children are held hostage," yelled Kim as the staff tried to bind her to a new chair.

"They will be released just as soon as people see the videos on how happy they are with us. After that, horrible images of children who were not protected against abuse. All because of a failed system."

"Justify your actions to the families of the twelve

missing children you have hidden in your underground structures."

"There are various comments about breaking eggs to cook an omelet."

"So kids are like eggs, to be broken when you deem necessary," spat out Audrey.

Samuel's face flushed with anger. "You're wearing out your welcome. You may not survive this incident if you must keep trying to push our buttons."

"You think killing an Agent will create more sympathy for your cause?" asked Kim.

"People will understand once they see our voluminous evidence."

Kim barked out a laugh. "Your understanding of the human condition is exceptionally flawed. Your martyr complex is very evident."

What the film world describes as an evil smile formed on Samuels's face. "When your children join others in our organization at a different location, we will see your response then."

"Are you crazy?" said Audrey.

"No, We realize we must keep this drama going as long as possible to prevent censorship or forgetfulness. We *will* get our message across—one way or the other."

Tim Weiss began to curse in more than one language.

"That damn message these wackos are broadcasting sounds more like Koesch and Waco at every sentence."

"They now use Kim and Audrey as hostages," added FBI supervisor Marcia Bernal. "Not to mention they still have the twelve children."

"I'll believe they are about to release the kids when I see it."

"Our HRT and WET teams are pinned down. We underestimated how violent these people could be."

"Hell, Marcia, the entire child abuse and trafficking community thought this World Education Group was the epidemy of morality. They had everyone snowed."

"Something pushed them over the edge early."

"I think, Marcia, two dead bodies, one a pedophile, forced their hands."

"Huh. I think the ease of the killings, the dismembering of the one body, shows they were already on edge."

"And our two Agents snooping pushed them over." Sam cursed some more. "If they hurt Kim and Audrey, I'll gut them with a dull fish knife."

"I'll hold them down for you," replied Marcia.

13.

Another oversized masked male, Baby Grizzly, was on the lookout on the wooden front porch armed with a semi-auto twelve gauge shotgun. He saw some movement about fifty yards down the driveway but did not react. The federal agents were fanning out sideways and not approaching any nearer. Baby Grizzly grinned under his mask. He knew the Mission Message was being broadcast and disseminated on every conceivable information platform. Thus, the World Overlord Government would be frozen in their response. The Dark Side could not stand the light, and the Mission was light, exposing the corrupt system that claimed to protect the innocent.

Baby Grizzly grimaced under his mask. No one ever protected him when he was a child. Only when he grew large then did people leave him alone.

A loud canine bark jerked him from his thoughts. A large white dog approached him from the surrounding trees, wagging its tail and with its muzzle in a doggy grin.

"Hey, girl. Where did you come from?"

Baby Grizzly liked dogs. He was never allowed to have one growing up.

The masked minion shifted his weapon and reached out to pet the oversized canine. Distracted, he did not see an equally large black shape dashing from the brush. Blackie slammed into the man's side and sent the shotgun flying. Snow joined her mate and clamped her jaws around the throat of the stunned sentry. Blood and oxygen shut off, and the man slipped into unconsciousness.

"Baby Grizzly's helmet camera just shut off," said Baby Raven. "Last image was him trying to pet a large white dog."

"A police K-9?' Asked Baby Raccoon.

"Too friendly. And no body armor. There was no handler around either. I don't see them sending a K-9 up to get shot."

"I'll go check."

Baby Racoon hefted her assault rifle. After the Grette fiasco, she would not let anyone at the compound come to harm—nor escape.

"Are those K-9s on the porch?" said a WET Agent.

"Not any of ours," replied the FBI Team Leader. "Must be theirs."

"I hope not. I don't want to shoot someone's innocent dog. Bastards."

John Richards was low crawling and hoping no surveillance cameras could see him coming in ninety degrees from the driveway and the delayed tactical teams. He had always been good at sneaky petering as a PJ. However, that was usually when the enemy was not on alert. The tactical teams' aborted entry ruined any chance of surprise.

"Where are the dogs?" he thought. Snow and Blackie were just too intelligent and independent for their own good.

Then Snow seemed to appear from nowhere. She pulled on his sleeve, then took off back towards the front porch of the residence. John scrambled to his feet.

"Shit. No use hiding now." The former PJ sprinted to the main entrance.

Baby Racoon opened the front entrance double doors a few inches. The first image which met her eyes was a prone Baby Grizzly. She reached for the shoulder-mounted radio microphone as she tried to survey the area. She saw a man running at her, and she squealed, dropped the microphone, and raised her assault rifle. Her peripheral visions did not register a sizeable black shape bounding at her until she was smashed onto the wooden porch. Her body camera went dark, as did her vision.

"Sonofabitch," swore the FBI Team Leader. "Those dogs are giving us an opening. All Team Members, Assault. This may be our only chance."

"What about that guy following them?" asked the WET Senior Agent.

"Text I received says to watch out for the dog's owner, a former USAF Vet. He's on our side."

"Well, he is about to be caught in a crossfire."

Before Richard could reach the open entrance doors, Snow and Blackie went through.

"Goddamn, it! Wait, you two."

Not for the first time did Richard wonder who was really in charge.

Two staff members tried to bind Kim to a new chair as they removed the remains of the smashed chai. Baby Gorilla attempted to staunch the bleeding from the face wound.

"You will pay for this, bitch," the big man mumbled."

"There has been a breach at the main entrance," Baby Raven called out.

"Well, lock down the access doors to the basement," ordered Samuel. "They are reinforced and should delay—"

"One stairway door smashed open before I could activate the heavy deadbolts."

"People, guns. Now."

The Neilson Twins had moved a dozen staff members to the main floor and the basement room. Two stayed with the now-drugged-to-sleep children in a deeper basement room. With two near the front entrance down and out, that left four effectives guarding the upper levels and six with Samuel and Samantha. As the two of them continued to rebind Kim, Baby Gorilla was staunching the blood from his wound. The other three went to a gun locker at the far end of the extended basement room. As they removed rifles and extended magazines, Audrey tested the bindings. Her right leg moved free as the chair leg broke.

Kim moved.

A kick to the face shattered the nose of a female minion as Kim jabbed the male, trying to restrain her in his eyes. Mama Tiger had woken.

Kim twisted and scissored her legs, righting herself to standing. A high kick flattened the male as Audrey said," You go, girl."

"*Shoot her,*" yelled Samantha. Her minions were not trained soldiers, so they fumbled to load their weapons under stress. Kim launched into a spinning movement more apt to be seen in an ice skating rink. As the Special Agent landed, she went into a forward roll and kicked herself at the three armed staff. As the nearest armed male raised his rifle, Kim collided with him in the personal space of all three armed individuals. At that moment, she became a Whirling Dervish.

Kicks, slaps, elbow strikes, and clawed fingers did the damage as Kim released feral screams of anger. How *dare* they threaten her children.

Audrey hopped on her free right leg and propelled herself backward at an angle. As she hit the hard floor, the chair broke apart.

Baby Gorilla forgot his injury, bellowed, and rushed at Kim. The practitioner of East Indian Martial Arts went low at the attacker's legs. Kim tripped the charging big man and quickly wrapped one of his limbs in a painful leg lock. A loud snap came in the blink of an eye, and Baby Gorilla screamed in pain. Kim scrambled to her feet and faced the Neilsen Twins.

"Your turn," she growled.

Samuel produced a hidden Taser and shot her. Thousands of volts of electricity knocked the Special Agent to the floor.

"Baby Fox, get our Grandfather's pistol."

Audrey tore herself from the broken chair and charged. The Taser was a single-shot variety, so all the Twin could do was stare just before Audrey slammed into him. The Taser went one way, and Samuel, with Audrey on top, went the other.

"You piece of shit," Audrey yelled as she punched the one known as Baby Bear.

The FBI Agent pummeled the kidnapper of children until his face was a bloody mess.

Kim was trying to regain her feet when she heard the recognizable 'pfttt' sound of a silenced pistol. She saw Samantha holding a long-barreled twenty-two caliber pistol with an attached silencer. Audrey rolled off Samuel holding her side as red stained her clothes.

"One more move, and I reshoot her. Then you."

The battered and bleeding Samuel lurched to his feet. "Now suffer the result of your actions, bitches." The Twin stumbled over to a desk, opened a drawer, and removed a four-inch-long cylindrical object.

"See this detonator?" The madman hissed through bloody lips and broken teeth. "I push the button on top, and we all go up in smoke."

"And the children? What about them?" asked Kim as she stood up.

"They should survive in a reinforced room below. Two medical trained staff are monitoring their drugged sleep." Then Samuel shrugged. "If not, they will be useful martyrs. You and the rest of the government must go to great lengths to explain how this happened." An evil grin formed on the damaged mouth. "This will be referred to as Waco Redux as other of our followers spread the Mission ideals."

"Now what," Audrey groaned from her position on the floor. A red stain was widening on her torso. "You going to talk us to death?"

"Agent Kupar, you will see to your partner. We will provide a medical kit to help keep her alive for longer. You make good additional hostages—"

No one could explain how the black and white blurred shapes made it to the basement unnoticed. Blackie's jaws crushed the wrist holding the detonator, almost amputating the hand. The unpushed detonator flew from Samuel's grasp, and Kim dove to catch it as Samuel shrieked in pain. Something stung the HSI Agent's side as she kept the detonator from hitting the ground. Then Samantha screamed. A crunching sound cut off the cry in mid-scream. A person cannot cry out when a large white dog has crushed their throat and larynx.

For a few moments, Blackie and Snow kept the minions from moving with vicious snarls. John Richards then came leaping down the stairs, pistol drawn. Seconds later, members of the Tactical Teams arrived,

"Hey people, we are both leaking Claret here," Audrey called out. "Is there a medic in the house?"

Kim looked at her side. There were widening spots of red on her blouse.

"Hank's going to be so pissed—" Then her vision went dark.

14.

Kim cried out and jerked awake. Completely disoriented, she cried out for her children. Then a female nurse's face hovered over her.

"Hello, Kim Kupar. You are in a hospital," said the middle-aged brown-haired woman. "Your husband and twins are well and will come back to visit you now that you are awake."

"How long—" with the rest of the question cut off by a straw in her mouth.

"Sip on this water," said the nurse." Your throat is dry, I bet." The nurse was correct. Water never tasted so good. "To answer your question, you have been out for the count for two days. We chased your husband away a few hours ago."

"I need to breastfeed—"

"The doctor had us use a breast pump on you to

relieve the buildup when your nipples began to leak. However, the milk has some painkillers, so I don't think young children should drink it."

"Agent DiStefano—Audrey. How is she?"

"Better than you. She took one of those nasty exploding bullets like the ones declared illegal after Reagan was shot. You took three."

The pain set in at the mention of the wounds. The nurse seemed to sense that fact. "I'm Nurse Karen Strong. I'll get you some pain meds, as you probably need them. Doctor Yee will be on rounds shortly and explain everything."

Nurse Strong obtained a syringe and administered the pain meds through an IV needle and tube still stuck in her arm. Kim soon felt the fuzzy lethargy that hard painkiller narcotics often produced. She wanted more information on what had happened and if the children were rescued without casualties. Kim tried to fight off the effects of the pain medication when she heard a familiar voice.

"Hey, Partner. You're awake."

Kim managed to turn her fuzzy-feeling head to see Audrey sitting in a wheelchair pushed by some nurse's aid. Tears clouded her already drugged vision as she smiled at the FBI Agent.

"I'm here, but not really awake, Audrey. I—" Kim began to cry. Audrey reached out and grabbed her hand.

"Hey, sister. We made it. The kids all made it. No

other Agents were hurt, and the Neilsens are out of circulation."

Kim controlled her tears and squeezed Audrey's hand. "I guess we made a pretty good team then."

"Yes, Tiger Lady. We took the only bullets, although one Hostage Rescue Team member took a steel rod through his leg."

"Did some of the WEG followers get to my home? Get to my twins?"

Audrey took Kim's hand in both of hers. "They tried. And this ole retired dinosaur you call T-rex showed up as a guardian angel. Two miscreants are pushing up daisies, with Hank obtaining a short headache from a Taser."

"Someone up there must like me."

"You have a way with beasties, Kim, that is for sure. The Richard's dogs showed up at just the right time."

"Audrey, I owe so many people so much. I have such great friends."

"Hey, Partner. That's what friends and family do—they have your back."

Kim's eyelids became even heavier. "Audrey, I'm drifting"—Then Kim was asleep.

The FBI Agent wiped tears from her eyes. "You sleep the sleep of the good and innocent, my best friend, Kim. You deserve it." Audrey looked at the nurse's aide. "My broken rib is beginning to hurt again. I guess it's time to wheel back to my room."

"Is she the Tiger Lady from the newspapers?" asked the young lady.

"That she is. You just met a legend. Now, please, back to my bed. This Former Marine needs to rest."

Doctor Yee woke Kim up two hours later. He explained the extent of her injuries.

"Everything still works, young lady. The three exploding bullets, although small, spread a bunch of tiny shrapnel in your body. You may have some small scars, but I ensured no lasting internal damage."

"I can still have additional children?" asked Kim

"Yes. I double-checked what people call your female parts. Nothing was hurt."

"Thank God. And thank you, Doctor."

Doctor Yee smiled. "You get some more rest. I will contact your husband so he may visit you in a few hours. For now, you rest, Agent Kupar. Doctor's Orders."

Before Kim drifted off to sleep again, she wondered how many criminal World Education Group were hospitalized. Most were probably in a lock-up somewhere. However, seeing Samuel lose a hand to a powerful canine bite and Snow crushing Samantha's throat made Kim wonder who did survive. She doubts the Doctor would tell her specifics due to medical records privacy regulations and laws.

"Hope they suffer and feel fear," Kim thought just

before drifting off. *"They all deserve a special Hell for taking the children."*

Law Enforcement Forensics Psychiatrist Charles Brown did not stand up when they brought the shackled Samuel Neilsen into the secure interview room at the Kitsap County Jail. The Sheriff's Deputies had produced some interesting shackles as the prisoner's right hand was in a massive cast. The hospital medical staff attempted to save Samuel's hand, with only time telling if they were successful.

The Jail Staff shackled the left hand to the restraint ring on the table before they nodded to Charles and left the room.

"Mister Neilsen, I understand your attorney explained who I am and why I want to interview you."

"Yes, Doctor. You are a former law enforcement officer who is now a psychiatrist and often works at the behest of the court system," Samuel replied. "You want to decide if I am sane enough to stand a criminal trial. Or, if I am deemed crazy enough, to start the process to commit me to some secure mental health facility such as Western State until I become magically sane."

"You and your legal representative agreed to this recorded interview in writing before the Deputies brought you here. Correct?"

"Yes, Doctor. For the recorded record, that is true."

"So, to formally start this process, it is 9:30 AM on the agreed upon date, at a secure interview room in the Kitsap County Jail and Detention Center. I am Doctor Charles Brown, sitting as the film will show across from Samuel Neilsen."

"Excuse me, Doctor, but may I ask a question before you begin your examination?"

"Yes, if it is within certain bounds."

"May I ask—did my sister Samantha survive? I heard she did not. I also sense she did not."

"Your legal counsel was officially advised that she is deceased."

"Yes, he said such. I just wanted to hear it from a law enforcement representative and on tape."

"So, as part of this examination, how does your sister's death make you feel?"

Samuel 'Baby Bear' Neilsen stared at Charles. "Angry, of course. As well as sad. And also satisfied that Samantha is the first great martyr of our Mission."

"So the broadcasts you made and written statements on the Internet about your mission involving exposing how children, specifically orphans and foster children, are treated, still reflect your basic belief system."

"Why, of course, Doctor. One does not become a coward and give up basic truths just because of the possibility of death."

"Currently, Washington State has no operational

Death Penalty."

Baby Bear laughed. "They will find a way. Remember Epstein. The One World Government and federal agencies would dare not allow such embarrassing information about their inadequacies to be spread. Imprisonment of my followers and I will not prevent the truth from spreading."

"What do you believe will result from spreading your truth worldwide, Samuel?"

Baby Bear's facial features formed into a Death's Head grin. "You reap what you sow, Doctor. You reap what you sow."

Kim woke up to the sound of babies happy gurgling. Her eyes finally focused on a large bearded man grinning and holding two gurgling babies.

"Hey. Mom's awake," said Hank.

Kim slowly sat up and reached her hands out to her twins. The motion made her stitches pull, but she ignored the pain. Her children were here to hug.

"Come to Momma, kids."

Hank held the twins out to Kim. Rex and Guadalupe gurgled and giggled as they grasped Kim with their growing hands. Kim snuggled her face into the short hair of the twins and took a deep breath. All was right with the world when a mother could smell her children.

"What have you been doing for milk, Hank? I still

can't breastfeed; I have too many painkillers in my system."

"High-quality formula seems to be working. Your mother is arranging for wet nurses if necessary."

"Leave it to my mother to go Old School on us. I don't even know if wetnurses are a 'thing' anymore."

"Well, we'll work it out. I want to get you home. The kids and I miss you."

"Just as soon as Doctor Yee allows me, I am gone."

Hank bent over and kissed his lover. "I would like you to have a nice long break from fieldwork, Kim. I don't want any more bullet holes in my wife."

"That is being taken care of, Hank," came from a voice in the doorway. ASAC Tim Weiss stood at the door with a bouquet and fruit basket. "A Jew is bearing gifts from your fellow employees. And, yes, Hank, ICE headquarters, has an idea to use Kim's unique talents while giving her a rest from the field." Tim handed the flowers to Kim as Hank recovered the twins.

"They smell nice, Sir. But my babies smell nicer."

The ASAC grinned. "Mothers like the smell of their babies and can often tell if they are ill."

"You have children," said Hank.

"Guilty as charged. So yes, I am sensitive to Kim and your situation. "

"So before I get drowsy again, what do you have in mind, Sir?" asked Kim.

"Someone in Headquarters thought your experience and language abilities might be of help at the Federal Law Enforcement Training Center in Brunswick, Georgia. That would be for Homeland Security training and any other Agency or Department attending training. It would include some State and Local agencies also."

Hank and Kim sat silent as the twins cooed and gurgled as they held onto their often absent mother. "Sir, I can't leave my family, children, and home right after being in the hospital—"

"Who said anything about leaving your family? Housing will be arranged for them to stay with you, and we can help rent your home here out. Or maybe a relative could move in."

"Where are the funds for all this?" asked Hank. "I know Temporary Duty Assignments have decent per diem, but we have a mortgage, car payment, and medical costs for our Twins."

ASAC Weiss sat in an available chair and fixed his gaze on the twins.

"As an extended honorary Uncle to the little ones, you can be assured that I will do everything to keep them happy and you two safe and secure. Thus, I did some politicking with the powers that be. Kim, you and your family will be cared for decently. The reason is that you and Audrey are heroes. You returned twelve unharmed children of color to their families and caught the assholes who took them."

"But if not for those crazy dogs, the tactical team, and the Richards—"

"Stop right there. Who found the Neilsens? Who put two and two together and tracked them down? Do you both realize this is one of the few cases where the FBI and ICE worked together without a dogfight? The positive press from the Rainbow Investigation will continue for months. *That* gives us political capital to find the money and will to get you into a training position where I know you will do an excellent job."

Kim snuffled the twins some more as she thought. She had never considered being the instructor rather than the student. However, being an instructor would be suitable for promotions and getting her out of the field. She looked at Hank.

"What do you think? Having someone live in our house, keep it up?"

"Anything that gives you more time with the twins and keeps you from dodging bullets and other dangers is okay with me." Hank gently stroked his wife's hair.

"You are also an excellent example of what a person can accomplish when they put their mind to it. I often wonder why you married an also-ran like me."

Kim blinked back tears as she answered. "You are the love of my life, and we have two beautiful children together. Yet you still question whether we were made for each other. Stop it."

Kim looked the ASAC in the eye. "If you can swing it, you have a deal. After I heal a bit more, of course."

The ASAC smiled as he answered. "Of course. My contacts at the FBI also say you and Audrey may need to visit Quantico for some briefings at the FBI Academy. Plus, Mean Green wants you to explain to their basic U.S. Border Patrol Classes the importance of bilingual abilities in federal investigations. I hear Artesia; New Mexico is pleasant in the Fall and Winter."

"No rest for the wicked, I see," said Kim. "Is Audrey still in the hospital?"

"I heard she will be discharged tomorrow. I imagine she will stop by before she leaves."

"She'd better, or I will hobble around and beat her with my crutches."

The adults laughed at the thought as the twins giggled and gurgled in happiness.

Early the following day, Kim was trying to open her eyes when a familiar voice came from the doorway.

"Hey, Pard. How you're doing."

Audrey stood grinning as she spoke.

"Well, Audrey, you are on two feet, even with a cane, so you are better off than I am."

The FBI agent limped into the room, went to

Kim's bedside, and hugged her.

"We made it, Lady. We made it."

Audrey blinked back tears as Kim kissed her on the cheek.

"I guess you and I are destined for other things," said Kim.

Audrey stood up from the hug and wiped away a tear. "You must have received a similar speech from your bosses."

"Yes, Audrey. It sounds like they want to put us at least temporarily out to the training pasture. Which is okay for me, the kids, and Hank. How about you?"

Audrey shrugged. "Machts nichts. It's all for twenty, as they say. However, we must still help put the surviving minions and Samuel Neilsen away. Trials will be coming up in the next months."

"True. We'll have to write reports on what happened to us. Plus, testimony before a Federal Grand Jury and in various courts."

"So, maybe after you are released, we can sit on your back patio and sip margaritas while we write the necessary reports. We will both be on sick leave or lite duty for a while."

Kim laughed, which pulled her stitches. "Maybe. By the way, why the cane? I thought you were shot in the side."

"Being slapped around in the chair injured one of my legs. Physical therapy is required."

"Well, then. I guess the Gimp Squad is in shape for report writing and not much more. I think between us, we can swing that assignment."

"Shake, Pard. I think we have it figured out."

15.

Two days later, Kim was released from the hospital. Doctor Yee felt she was out of the woods for any danger of infection. ASAC Weiss talked to his FBI counterpart, Marcia Bernal, and arranged for the two Agents to work remotely at Kim's home.

"Hell, if we did some during COVID, why not now?" Weiss said.

The high-end defense attornies for World Education Group lept into high gear within twenty-four hours of the raid and arrests. While Charles Brown was interviewing and examining Samuel Neilsen for mental competency to stand trial, the vast supporting connections of the group began a campaign of defense. The raid was by jack-booted thugs who misunderstood what the WEG stood for in child protective organizations. Audrey and Kim were psychotic liars involved in a Lesbian relationship. Samuel's sister Samantha was torn to pieces by vicious dogs as law enforcement stood by and laughed. The staff and the Neilsens suffered from long-term PTSD, partly caused by childhood abuse and increased by a corrupt system. It was another Waco where the children were lucky to be alive.

The defense came to a screeching halt when Samuel broadcasted a statement against his lawyers' wishes.

"I will not attempt to defend our actions based on mental incompetency. Nor will I claim that our staff and I did not understand the results of our efforts. Nor will I blame it on my dead sister; we did what we did because it was the *right* path. We removed children from an abusive society and showed them love and affection they had never known before. We are rescuers, not kidnappers." Samuel paused, then continued. "The world's citizens will see that we harmed no one other than when defending the children and ourselves. Three of our comrades, including my sainted Twin, were killed. I look forward to our day in court when the Truth Shall Set Us Free."

Forensic psychiatrist Charles Brown visited Kim and Audrey and briefed them on his findings.

"In the street vernacular, Samuel is bug nuts."

"However," Charles continued, "he admits he and the others knew right from wrong, even if they are convinced their actions are right."

"Then, with no insanity defense, it should be a slam-dunk case," Kim stated.

"Hell, they want a show trial, so they will still claim they are not guilty and file motions to admit their defense of good against evil government actions. And our justice system will allow them to claim they are not guilty initially until a judge dismisses the defense motions, Watch for antics like the Manson Family in history. Samuel wants to be a martyr."

"How will any judge worth their salt allow a self-defense plea?" asked Audrey.

"Even if a judge disallows it, this may involve a federal death penalty charge. Thus, all the defendants will initially receive a 'not guilty' plea on their behalf. Plus, based on the politics of the situation, a judge may be empathetic to some of the motions made for specific defendants. WEG and its supporters will argue that the ends justify the means in the media and court and require each defendant to be tied directly to each action, even with conspiracy charges. Even if they admitted to killing the pedophile, would people consider that a problem? It fits into the idea that 'it was all for the children'."

"So them hurting Hank and trying to steal my Twins does not count for much," added Kim.

"It will be up to the AUSA and local DAs who will

be charged with what. You and Audrey heard Samuel state he and his sister planned to take your children. Then members of their group attempted, so we have reasonable conspiracy charges against Samuel and the one survivor. The rest of the staff will claim ignorance until Samuel tells you of the plan."

"The rest of the staff at least were involved in the abduction of the thirteen children of color. They are part of the greater conspiracy."

Charles sighed and then spoke. "I and others get to perform complete psychological workups on the so-called staff. They will try to claim various forms of PTSD from years of abuse as mitigating factors."

"But they still kidnapped children."

"Hey, everyone will play the victim card. After all, society and Child Protective Services are at fault. The Devil made them do it."

Audrey shook her head. "Man, I am so glad I got a chance to beat on Samuel. It was worth a bullet to the ribs."

The Defense Counsel for all the defendants waived Initial Appearances/Probable Cause Hearings and requested a speedy trial for all involved. This action led Senior Special Agent Richard Johnson to telephone Kim and Audrey as they reviewed case information at Kim's home.

"I don't want to butt in your case; however, with your permission, I would like to take a crack at the

Doctor referred to as Baby Rabbit."

"We are still trying to lock down her real name and identity, Richard. She supposedly has a medical license but has no fingerprints in any system we reviewed."

"I know. Charlie Brown and I would like to interview her. Maybe we can convince her that her medical ethics require her to cooperate."

Kim and Audrey both laughed at the speakerphone. "What medical ethics?" Audrey interjected. "She kept young children doped up on happy juice after kidnapping them."

"Indications are she expressed some concern about the continual use of drugs to control the children, so there may still be ethics floating around her brain. Plus, I have some special contacts who may help me discover how she became a non-person."

"Have at it, Richard. It will be interesting to see if the lawyers let you anywhere near her."

Richard Johnson and Charles Brown watched as the Bureau of Prisons Officers escorted the woman known as Baby Rabbit into the secured interview room at the Federal Detention Center SEATAC, Washington. The lawyer, Mrs. Robinson, came in with the alleged doctor of medium height and build. The prison jumpsuit with BOP stenciled on the back did not distract from the late thirties brown-haired woman's fundamental attractiveness.

As the BOP officers ensured that Baby Rabbit would be secure with the law enforcement officials, Richard smiled and said, "Hello, Kelly Parsons. I guess you kept up with your medical duties until you wound up here."

"That is not my client's legal name, Agent. Baby Rabbit is her legal name on record."

"Oh, cut the crap, counselor. Kelly Parsons is whom we are talking with now. We have a remarkable record for her, *not* Baby Rabbit."

"That claim is the only reason my client is here, "said a frowning Mrs. Robinson. "So, should we cut to the chase and present the documents which pertain to her? I don't want some fantasy released to the public to influence the future hearings and trial."

Richard laughed.

"What's so funny?" demanded Mrs. Robinson.

"Rather than sit here, trade jibes and comments, here is a declassified file. Please pay particular attention to the photographs. As they say, a picture is worth a thousand words."

The attorney opened the file and examined the photos. Her mouth dropped open, and she stared at Kelly Parsons, AKA Baby Rabbit. The doctor.

"What?" the prisoner said as she reached for the file. Within ten seconds, the doctor for WEG turned towards Richard and Charles.

"Where did you get these photos?" she asked.

"When I explained to some of the high-security contacts that I was involved in the investigation of the kidnapped children of color, they quickly began a search and declassification of this—information."

Richard leaned forward towards Parsons.

"As embarrassing as this project you were involved in was for some people at the top of the food chain, no one wants to be tied in with concealing child abuse and torture."

"Where were those photographs taken?" asked the attorney. "And how do I know they were not created from whole cloth?"

"Kelly knows they were real, don't you, Baby Rabbit."

Mrs. Robinson glared at her client. "What the Hell do you have me involved in? I signed on to help based on my experience through Polaris with the WEG. If it turns out you were involved in this... *sickness?* Color me gone."

"Come on, Kelly. Tell your lawyer what those photos and that file are all about. Come on, *tell her.*"

The former medical professional sat silent for a moment. Then, Parsons began to talk as tears ran down her cheeks. "I was assigned to a special operations group. Take Abu Ghraib prison in Iraq and expand it to include all the enemies of the United States. That includes Narco Trafficantes, world slavers, sex traffickers, and pedophile rings. Some people at the—

highest level decided to go after the families of some of these 'enemies' and criminals."

"Who made up this enemies list?" asked Charles.

"Some people at a pinnacle or apex level in the stratosphere of government. I was just a soldier, a cog in a large machine created to deal with the evils you mentioned."

"You were a doctor who took an oath. Remember, 'do no harm' in medical school?"

Kelly Parsons could not meet his gaze. "We were told the people we were dealing with were a threat to hundreds, thousands of innocents."

"So you took the families, the children of these— targets- and tortured them for information and cooperation. Correct?"

The woman known as Baby Rabbit said nothing. Charles slammed the hook that replaced his hand due to an IED on the table. Both the women jerked in their chairs.

"Answer me!"

"Yes. Oh my God, yes. I sold my soul," sobbed Kelly. "When I heard about the Neilsens and WEG, I thought this was a way to atone for my sins."

"Did they know of your background?" asked Richard. Kelly nodded 'yes,' as Charles handed her a Kleenex with his good hand.

"Yet they hired you anyways? All the other staff members, their minions, had histories of abuse while in the foster child system or suffered at the hands of family members. Why would they accept you into their group?"

"They knew I had been a talented medical professional at one time. I was at the top of my medical class in pediatric medicine. They said as such."

"That still means they were violating the principles of their alleged mission. I thought they wanted people who abused children to be punished and not allowed into the child care system."

"They said my talents outweighed my wrongdoing. That I could cleanse my spirit of what I did and saw." The woman, also named Baby Rabbit, looked at the floor. "Then they said they would need my experience and talents at—information gathering. They said they might need my talents at influencing and obtaining cooperation from people who stood in the way."

"In other words, using threats and force if necessary."

"Yes," mumbled Kelly.

"I think in my client's best interests, we need to end this interview," said Mrs. Robinson. "The shock of this new—information made me forget my responsibility as her attorney for a moment."

"Fine," said Richard as he began to stand. "We have enough to crucify Kelly Parsons just from the now declassified file and the evidence of her keeping the children pliant thanks to a lot of happy juice."

The licensed doctor looked directly at Richard. "I need to tell you something else."

"As your lawyer, I cannot allow—"

"Shut up!" snapped Kelly. She fixed her gaze on the Senior Special Agent. "The Neilsens planned on taking Kim Kupar's twins not just as leverage. They planned on making them—suffer."

"Why?"

"A part of them wants psychotic revenge on everyone associated with authority. If you double-check the information on the children taken, a couple were from influential families with ties to local government. That information was lost in the shuffle of having thirteen unrelated children taken, with no ransom notes or ZODIAC killer-like letters."

"So if the situation had continued—"

"They would also—suffer."

"And you would help keep them alive and help in the suffering," said Charles.

"Yes." She stared at the two law enforcement officials. "This is not over because this group is in jail. The Neilsens have other contacts still free. They are the type who will do most anything for money, which WEG has hidden." Kelly looked towards the floor again. "I should have done something when I found out the Neilsens had an escape tunnel for only their use. And then the pre-set explosive—I should have realized just how sick the Neilsens were."

"So, anyone involved in this investigation is at risk of revenge?"

"Yes. Especially those involved in the death of Samantha. The fate of the others matters little to Samuel. Revenge matters most."

16.

Audrey and Kim were at the physical therapy complex contracted by the government for their care when Richard Johnson and Charles Brown walked in with four female Special Agents. Kim smiled as she recognized a large and good friend among them. Fish and Wildlife Agent Brenna Friberg's tall, blonde, and Nordic frame was immediately recognized.

"To what do I owe this visit, Brenna?"

"Richard asked that I come along," Brenna said with a grin, "and I hope I may see your twins."

"That can easily be arranged after Richard tells me what's up."

Richard Johnson stepped up to Audrey and Kim. "What's up is that you have an assigned protection detail from now on. I'll let you read this report of a recent conversation with the doctor known as Baby Rabbit."

He handed Kim and Audrey a copy of an ROI as two Special Agents led the physical therapists away from their clients. Future therapy would have to wait.

Five minutes later, Kim looked Richard in the eye. "Any chance Kelly Parsons is exaggerating?"

"Not when the escape tunnel was found. The Neilsens were not whom they portrayed."

"Did Baby Rabbit know of the escape tunnel for Samuel and Samantha?" Audrey asked.

"Yes. They told Kelly just before you showed up for the interview in Olalla. Their desire to be dead martyrs was all a show."

"What about the detonator?"

"That was real and would have killed the children and the staff watching them."

Kim looked at Charles Brown. "All this concern about children and child abuse. WEG was based on lies."

"They are stone-cold psychopaths. Yes, their adoptive parents were abusive. However, instead of helping abuse victims, they became victimizers. The victimization seems to be due to a sick desire for vengeance on society. All evidence points to them murdering their adoptive parent now that people look deeper into the deaths."

"And even though Samantha is dead and Samuel is locked up, we are still in danger?"

"They developed a network of outsiders who will

do what is asked. Samuel is still dangerous, with millions in hidden funds and treasure. The same psychotic behavior which led them to believe they had a natural right to do what they wanted to all of us little people also led them to make stupid mistakes. Like leaving the body of the pedophile at their leased property in Tacoma. They thought rules didn't apply to them and that no one would notice strange activities until it was too late and the trail was cold."

Audrey chuckled a response. "And a lady of the evening reported something which led Kim and me to discover the body early."

"Yes. No one would have noticed the corpse until it started to stink. The landlord said he rarely visited them."

"Richard, I guess the Assistant U.S Attorney in charge of this case will want to talk to all of us, "said Kim.

"Yes. Kathy Mueller won't mind you showing up in your workout clothes. However, we must get this all before a federal grand jury at the soonest opportunity."

"So, what about Hank and the twins?"

"A particular retired Senior Special Agent is sitting on your house until you get home with your security detail. The Richards will also receive a protection detail. Their dogs are targets for hate."

Kim took a deep breath and let it out. "No rest for the innocent, I see."

"Kim, Samuel said you reap what you sow," said

Charles. "In this case, we need to ensure the harvester runs over Samuel and his minions, not us."

AUSA Kathy Mueller met the Agents at an HSI office conference room on Second Avenue in Seattle. An attractive bronze-haired woman with freckles and a fit physique, Kathy smiled as she shook hands with Kim and Audrey.

"I finally get to meet the Dynamic Female Duo," she said with a welcoming grin. "I also get to meet the one called Tiger Lady in the AUSA office."

Kim hoped her natural tan hid the blush on her face. Audrey laughed and added to her embarrassment. "She has twin cubs now and still has a way with four-legged friends. Without two of them arriving at just the right moment—" Audrey left the rest of the statement hanging.

"Things worked out," interjected Kim. "Now, I guess the situation is even more complicated."

"Yes, it is," replied Kathy. "Kelly Parsons. AKA Baby Rabbit is providing state's evidence in return for protection and some federal prison time in a secret facility. Based on her previous participation in the hidden interrogation program Senior Agent Johnson helped uncover, the woman called Baby Rabbit will have to be held incommunicado for quite some time."

"Will she testify in open court?" asked Kim.

"Possibly, depending on the reaction of the other

defendants when their lawyers are provided with the Brady material. Everyone has separate counsel right now after it became apparent some defendants were more ignorant than others."

"Like the two guarding the children when Samuel produced the detonator. If he had managed to trigger the explosives, the staff members near the children could have been killed."

"Only Samuel, Samantha, and Kelly Parsons knew about the setup. And Kelly, AKA Baby Rabbit, only learned of the escape plans at the end."

"I bet some of the other staff members begin to roll over once they find out about the big lie," Audrey interjected.

"That is the hope. We need a Manson Style trial like a hole in the head. The best outcome is to keep them split up so we can concentrate on the surviving kingpin. There is still a Federal death penalty for some terror-related crimes, not to mention using deadly force on federal agents."

"So, what do you need from us?" asked Kim.

"Add more remembered details to your case reports and prepare for being grilled by defense attornies." Kathy Mueller paused for a moment, then continued.

"Plus, stay safe. Put up with having your version of the Secret Service twenty-four hours a day."

"So Richard Johnson's information is

not exaggerated."

"No, it is not. Samuel, through WEG, has the power of a small and very vicious state, like North Korea." Kathy Mueller slid a report toward the Agents.

"New findings on the death of their adoptive parents. Cut brake lines—then the two teenagers watched them bleed out before calling for help."

"Why no prosecution then?" asked Audrey.

"Poor kids in shock as they watched the car slam into the wrought iron access gate, which for some reason, the motor was frozen shut."

"Money talks, bullcrap walks."

"They and their adoptive Uncle had tons of it. No love was lost between the parents and the uncle who became their guardian."

"So Uncle John may have been in on it."

"Which resulted in him having a nasty accident with a snow plow."

Kim cringed as she spoke. "How in the hell did they hide all this psychotic behavior?!"

"Remember Ted Bundy? Imagine if he were fraternal twins."

Two days later, AUSA Kathy Mueller met defendant Samuel and his lawyer at a secured interview room at the Federal Detention Center. Richard Johnson and Charles Brown accompanied her to observe the reactions of the accused to new evidence gleaned from the statements of

Kelly Parsons.

"I thought I'd let you know early about the information the person you know as Baby Rabbit gave us," said Kathy as she slid a file to Stan Waterhouse, Samuel's attorney.

"I have already shared it with other defendants and ensured they obtained their chosen lawyers. The federal government is severing as many prosecutions from Samuel here to allow them to create independent agreements with my office."

"In other words, you want as many as possible to roll on their former leader, I believe is the street vernacular," replied Waterhouse.

"Read the file, counselor. You will see it is in their best interests not to trust Samuel after discovering a major set of lies told them."

Samuel and his lawyer examined the statements in the file for several moments. Then Samuel smiled as she spoke. "You will believe her lies to obtain a plea from me. You probably wish for me to plead to some insanity or mental defect and thus have no show trial."

"Not a show trial, Mister Neilsen. Instead, I want to avoid a circus. I will not allow a Manson-style fiasco with loyal minions parading and demonstrating before the Federal Courthouse. Spending millions for security so that you can rant on is not in the cards."

"So you think a jury will believe Baby Rabbit over me."

"Oh, cut the crap, Sam," interjected Richard. "We found the escape tunnels you built for you and your sister. Funny how the only person you informed about them was Kelly Parsons. And you did that as the Special Agents were coming to interview you."

"As a ruse for a Waco-style assault," said Waterhouse. "I am drafting motions to suppress evidence obtained from the illegal search and seizure."

Richard laughed. "You grabbed and hogtied Kima and Audrey, but that was all due to jackbooted thugs coming to arrest you for nothing. The twelve children were all there for a vacation."

"My client will let the jury hear the reasons for Samuel's and Samantha's actions. They can decide if their actions were warranted in light of society's failings to protect children from a failed child welfare system."

"Read the file carefully, Counselor," said Kathy. "All surviving staff involved are notified about the Neilsen's knowledge of Kelly Parson's background. They employed a government-sanctioned abuser in violation of the affirmed principles of WEG. They know of the escape tunnels which were not for them. They know the explosives would kill or maim the children and the two staff guarding them while the Neilsens fled out in the other direction."

The AUSA leaned closer to Samuel. "Kelly will also testify to the authenticity of some texts and emails you probably thought were gone. HSI computer forensics people are quite good. They outline your plan to abuse Agent Kupar's children for sick revenge against the so-called One World Government. How noble and sane are those concepts!"

Samuel flashed a feral grin at Charles Brown. "So, Doctor. Will you testify that I am insane, mentally incompetent? That would avoid a death sentence."

"Samuel, I would say you have some serious mental issues. Some may be due to the abuse you and your sister suffered from foster and adopted parents."

Charles paused, then continued. "However, you know right from wrong, even though you do not realize you're locked in the abused-abuser-abused cycle. You justify your actions with the pain you and others suffered. That failure to deal with your mental issues has led to the death and destruction of many innocent lives."

Samuel kept a smile on his face as he replied. "When you fight a war against an evil system, sometimes things are broken, and people die."

"Like your sister?"

The smile disappeared in a flash. "People will pay for that death."

"Ah, yes, another threat," interjected Richard Johnson. "More fodder for the jury to hear."

"This interview is over," stated Waterhouse. "I will see you all in court."

"I am going to the University of Washington Medical Center tomorrow," said Samuel. "Unlike you,

Doctor, I will have a hand, not a hook."

"Having two hands does not mean you have a soul, Samuel," replied Charles. "I think someday you will realize the sacrifice of a hand would be better than the sacrifice of your soul- and your sister."

Samuel growled like an angry dog and seemed ready to spit. His lawyer's hand on his arm stopped that.

"That is enough. Now, time for my client and I to have a private conference."

The Bureau of Prisons personnel escorted Samuel and his attorney to another secured room as the AUSA sat with the senior agent and the doctor.

"Despite all the evidence, this is not a slam dunk," said Kathy.

"Yep," replied Richard. "All it will take is one anti-government juror for a hung jury. World Education Group has a good reputation among many private organizations."

"Well, Polaris and the National Center For Missing & Exploited Children are quickly distancing themselves from Samuel and his subsidiary groups. There are already approved seizure warrants for funds and property connected to WEG and Samuel.

"You know he will have a lot of hidden assets, especially offshore.

"Well, Richard, that is for HSI and the FBI to track down. We must ensure we cut the heads off of all the snakes.

Charles sighed and stood up. "So many innocent children will be screwed over in this mess. Kids that WEG and its subsidiaries helped find new homes and new lives will be put through the wringer of the media and questions by their neighbors.

"Charles, Samuel, Samantha, and the company commented about breaking eggs for an omelet."

"Yes, the sick bastard," Charles looked hard at the others.

"It will be up to people like me to put them back together again."

Kathy Mueller had a fitful night of sleep. Her mind kept running a line from an old children's nursery rhyme.

"All the king's horses and all the king's men couldn't put Humpty together again."

Instead of an image of Humpty Dumpty, Kathy kept thinking of young Grette. Could she and the others be put back together again?

17.

Kim frowned as she ended the cell phone call with Richard Johnson. She had hoped pressure from the new information gleaned from Kelly Parsons would have caused some plea deal. Now Kim realized that hoping for some sanity involving Samuel Neilsen was unrealistic.

Giggling and gurgling from her twins quickly replaced the frown with a grin. Agent Brenna Friberg was laughing as she played "Peek-a-Boo" with the twins, who were ecstatic with the tall and blonde new playmate. Kim had seen the Special Agent in action and knew Brenna's reputation as a no-nonsense and tough law officer. You did not want to get on her wrong side. Then one saw Brenna around children. It was like two different people.

"Brenna, I think you have some hidden talents in child-rearing."

The tall-sometimes-Valkyrie grinned at her friend. "The Norskie community loves children. And I never really grew up when it came to playing games."

"So, is your biological clock ticking?"

Brenna, still grinning, shrugged. "You have to find Mister Right. Not just Right Now. Seeing you, Hank, and your twins make me think. Women in law enforcement have to plan well ahead for the time spent being pregnant. Having a supportive husband like Hank helps."

"My ears are burning," said Hank as he entered the room.

"Brenna was singing your praises as being a good husband and pack leader," replied Kim with a smile.

"Well, things will be easier once this Rainbow investigation is over," said Hank. "Then maybe some time as an instructor in Georgia."

"I hope you plan to return here," said Brenna. "I am always ready to spoil the kids."

"We plan on keeping the house," replied Kim. "If you know anybody who would want to rent while we are in FLETC, let me know."

"Hmmm," replied Brenna. "I'll have to think about that. Maybe I will move in. Then I can have more influence on your return."

"Well, based on what Richard Johnson told me on

the phone, we won't leave for a while. Samuel Neilsen and company will try to drag things out and create a circus. After Richard relates the information on the doctor we knew as Baby Rabbit to the other defendants, and she is cooperating, Samuel adopts a scorched earth tactic. All the defendant's cases are now severed with separate lawyers and trials. Some of his former minions will plead out; others will scream and point at Baby Bear and Baby Fox."

"No honor among child grabbers, I see," said Brenna.

"Well, he controlled them like a Jim Jones or a Koresch. However, his psychosis led to some significant mistakes. Killing people draws attention."

"I hope he gets the death penalty. At least maybe the federal government will put him down like the mad beast that he is."

"Well, tomorrow, he goes for more medical aid as the government tries to save his hand."

"No sense to that," said Hank. "Save his hand so we can kill him later."

"That's the system," replied Kim. "When he is being held in confinement, the government is responsible for his well-being."

"Well, I hope they use extra security precautions while he is being transported," opined Brenna. "He had too many wackadoodle friends, from my understanding."

Samuel Neilsen, AKA Baby Bear, was woken up at Oh-Dark-Thirty for his trip to the University of Washington Medical Center. The Federal Bureau of Prisons assigned four of their most experienced (and most formidable) Transport Officers to the trip. In addition, the U.S. Marshal's Service put two Marshals in a trail car to watch for any attempted contacts by WEG supporters. Everyone in law enforcement knew the story of the Neilsens and their abilities.

The influence of many connected organizations and subcontractor companies meant Samuel could receive the best medical care. In addition, media reports pointed out that the Federal Government was concerned about any question that an alleged serial kidnapper would be allowed to suffer from undue pain and permanent disability before the person was convicted of any crime. Samuel's high-priced lawyers would use any excuse to attack the AUSA and claim unfair prosecution. Thus, when Samuel requested the University Medical Center be brought into the attempts at saving his hand, there was little pushback.

It was decided to use Highway 99/Aurora Avenue North as the primary route to the University District and the Medical Center. The transport vehicles passed the area of the landmark Space Needle in downtown Seattle without incident. As the transport van neared the easterly turn onto North 45th Street, the sole female

Transport Officer smiled at the belly-chained prisoner.

"Not long now, Mister Neilsen."

Samuel grinned back as he replied, "No, not long now at all."

The Mac Truck/Tractor slammed into the side of the transport van, propelling it into the Southbound Aurora Avenue North lanes. The minions who planned the crash had paid specific attention to the opening segment of the film *HEAT* and figured a Mack Truck would be perfect for immobilizing the Bureara of Prison vehicle. There was much more traffic in the North Seattle Area than in the Los Angeles-based film. However, the 'snatch' team had planned for all situations.

Two darkened SUVs motored up to the crash, followed by an ambulance. As the U.S. Marshall trail vehicle personnel responded and radioed for a response, three COVID-masked individuals stepped out of the first SUV and sieved the government vehicle and the two Marshals with automatic fire. The vehicle gas tank was penetrated with incendiary rounds and exploded in a ball of flame.

Three other armed and masked individuals moved quickly to the smashed-up transport van. The use of the Mack truck had almost done too much damage as the three WEG minions tried to reach Samuel. The vehicle driver was shot as the front seat escort sat stunned and injured from the impact of the heavy vehicle. The two officers sitting near Samuel had weathered the storm better than the two in front and grabbed for their weapons. A flashbang thrown through the driver's open window detonated in the confines of the van and stunned them. Two oversized individuals' powerful arms and hands yanked the sliding side door open, allowing a third figure to jump into the vehicle next to Baby Bear.

Samuel knew what to expect, braced himself for the initial impact, and then closed his eyes as he crouched as best he could. The belly chain and handcuffs prevented Samuel from covering his ears, but he remained conscious of what happened after the flashbang explosion. The lithe third figure used hand-held tasers against the necks of the stunned guards to incapacitate them even more. A razor-sharp blade cut Samuel free from the shoulder strap seat belt, and strong hands lifted him from the back of the van. In mere moments he was in the back of the ambulance. A doctor and former Special Forces-trained EMT removed the handcuffs and belly chain, then strapped him down on a gurney.

The siren of the ambulance began to blare as Samuel's hearing returned. He smiled and spoke to the doctor before they covered his face with an oxygen mask. "Hello, doctor. I am glad to be in your care."

"You paid enough," said the woman with a Russian accent. "Now, to a special secret place."

Samuel told the escape planners not to share any details with him should the authorities find out. He knew that others like Baby Rabbit would love to force information from him. He had seen the photographs of what she had done and knew there were many others like her. Samuel refused to be the reason any others who helped were harmed by the government.

Samuel smiled once more as an oxygen mask was adjusted on his face.

Revenge would be so sweet.

Tim Weiss arranged a conference call with FBI ASAC Marcia Bernal, AUSA Kathy Mueller, Richard Johnson, Kima, and Audrey. S Officer

"We have an escaped subject, two dead U.S. Marshalls, a dead Bureau of Prison Officer, and three more hospitalized officers, one in critical condition." The ASAC paused as he tried not to curse. "We completely underestimated Samuel and his contacts. We failed to realize the level of violence Samuel would employ to escape. I, for one, thought he wanted a show trial."

"He's a psychopath, sir," said Richard Johnson. "He just demonstrated his bonafide as such an individual."

"And now everyone is pointing fingers," said Marcia. "The U.S. Marshalls and BOP a feeling blindsided by the level of violence. They are screaming about why the FBI did not warn them of the dangers of WEG and Samuel.

"Any information gleaned from the weapons and

vehicles abandoned?" asked Richard.

"They were items stolen in the past or illegally imported. Everyone wore gloves, and nothing traceable was left behind. The attackers disappeared into sidestreets before police arrived. The locals are looking for a nearby stash house."

"Homeland Security is just as culpable in not noticing the true potential of the Neilsens," added Sam.

"Yes, but this started as an FBI investigation," replied Marcia. "The buck ultimately stops with us."

"Ma'am, what do you want us to do?" asked Audrey. "Kim and I are ready to jump back into the game."

The FBI ASAC laughed. "That has been already noted, Agent. However, as you and others are material witnesses, Washington is considering moving everyone to a secure location. One suggestion was Joint Base Fort Lewis-McChord."

"Are you serious?" interjected Kim.

"Deathly serious," replied Sam Weiss. "I can't remember when a criminal organization was able to attack federal agents and take back a prisoner." Now Sam did begin to curse, then stopped himself.

"It now seems Samuel and company are out for revenge, not just making a statement about the evils of child care in our society."

"I think they were always out to make others suffer," interjected Kim. "They want others to feel the pain they claim from abusive parents."

"Whom they killed, it seems," said Richard.

"Well, they got their wish," said Sam. "The entire childcare system is in national news. There is a movement for a federal plan to supersede all State and Local Child Protective Services. Some people want all adoption and foster care systems under federal control."

"That will be a nightmare in a new bureaucracy," said Richard. "Federal Agencies have enough problems to deal with, including human trafficking."

"Well, those decisions are above our pay grades," added Marcia.

"When will we hear about the decision to move us all to a secure location?" asked Kim.

"I think tomorrow will be decision day," replied the FBI ASAC. "So, you might have some bags packed just in case."

Kim cuddled with Hank on their bed as the twins slept in the nearby cribs. Brenna and another female agent, Donna Chou, swapped out security duties in the home's front room. Audrey DiStefano moved into the spare bedroom two days prior, making coordination on her and Kim's reports of investigation easier. She kept a low profile to give the married couple a private night in their home. Any day now, Hank and Kim could be required to leave their comfortable home to live with their children in some secure government location. Time in their own bed could be a nostalgic memory after tomorrow.

"We'll get through this, Kim," said Hank as he squeezed his wife affectionally.

"I know, my love," Kim replied. "We are tough and make a good team."

"Are you looking forward to a break as an instructor after this case is completed?"

"Yes, Hank. I just wish I did not have to leave my home and nearby family. Georgia is completely across the United States. I hope the year or so at FLETC passes quickly."

"The time will pass faster than you realize. It always does when you're busy."

Kim looked up from her husband's muscular shoulder. "Will you be able to keep busy? You won't even have the Woodland Park Zoo to visit."

Hank kissed Kim, then answered. "I'll have the twins to keep me busy. We can explore the area and discover all flora and fauna. There are alligators in the Okefenokee Swamp. I can show the twins—"

"You keep them away from beasties like that. Take them to a dog park instead."

"Speaking of dogs, when we move back here, it will be time to get our kids a nice protective dog."

"Like the Richards' Snow or Blackie?"

"They may be able to make some suggestions. Snow and Blackie seem—unique."

"They have a Sir Kahn look in their eyes. They

have different intelligence.”

Hank gave Kim an affectionate squeeze. “You miss your big cat friend, don’t you, Tiger Lady.”

“Yes. Sir Kahn is special. He became a furry guardian angel for me at times. And, he brought us back together.”

Hank kissed Kim once more. “I love you, Tiger Lady.”

“And I, you, my modern Hercules.”

Something huge crashed into the front entranceway. Kim heard Brenna yell out, and then there were gunshots. Kim rolled out of bed, went straight to her pistol lockbox, and thumbed in the combination. Hank grabbed a Louisville Slugger he kept near the bed and went to the twin cribs at the bottom of the bed.

Audrey appeared at the bedroom door in her skivvies with a twelve gauge pump shotgun. “Stay with your kids!” The FBI Agent called out as she strode towards the front room.

Something roundish and dark broke through the bedroom window, and Hank fielded it like a baseball line drive. One quick throw and the object was in the backyard. Kim closed her eyes as she recognized it as a flashbang a moment before it detonated. The remaining window glass was blown around the room as a surprised cry emanated from the backyard.

“Hank, cover the twins,” Kim called out as she

approached the glassless window. Shadows moved in the dark, and Kim snapped off a round at one. To Hell with positive target identification; her children were in danger. Hank scooped up the now-screaming children and took them to the carpet with him. After the previous attempt at grabbing the twins, he and Kim had discussed what to do. Hank was to get the little ones to safety as soon as possible, while Kim provided firearm-backed cover.

A full-fledged firefight erupted in the front rooms. Kim crouched near Hank and her children as bullets penetrated the bedroom wall. Kim thought she heard Brenna cursing in Norwegian while Audrey let out some Marine warcry. Kim knew that the two protection agents assigned to Audrey would respond from a nearby motel, plus local law enforcement. Every law enforcement official had been notified of the situation after T-Rex had helped thwart the previous snatch job. Now Kim realized they were after her and Audrey, to be terminated with extreme prejudice.

There was a lull in the shooting, and Kim called out. "Hey, status report, people."

"We're still here!" Brenna loudly replied. "My vest stopped a round, and I will have another bruise. Chou and Audrey are okay."

"How about the assholes?"

"I think they left or are regrouping—"

Shooting began again as someone still had

murder in their minds. Kim watched as Hank covered the twins with his body and heard the clattering of an HSI MP-5 submachine gun firing frangible ammunition to prevent over-penetration in suburbia. The minions of Samuel were treating this situation as a free-fire zone just to get to Kim and Audrey.

Police and fire sirens added to the cacophony of sounds as added help arrived. Loudspeaker-enhanced commands of *"Police. Federal Agents. Drop your weapons!"* added to the din surrounding the home— more shots, some from a large caliber rifle, and then silence.

"Police Team coming in!" someone called out, and Kim knew the cavalry had arrived. She looked over at Hank and noticed a red stain on his nightshirt.

"Hank, you're hurt!"

Hank looked at Kim and then at where she was pointing. "Ah, Hell. Just a scratch. I can't feel it."

"Get me an EMT back here. My husband's been shot."

Hank was loaded into the back of an ambulance as Kim and Brenna tried to calm down the twins. An SUV smashing into the front door and followed by gunfire was not conducive to the rest and relaxation of very young children. The bullet which struck Hank had scraped across his broad shoulders and then embedded in the bedroom wall. He was taken to the nearby hospital as a precaution, even as Hank complained that it was just a scratch and he was alright.

ASACs Weiss and Bernal arrived and surveyed the situation. "Needless to say, Kim, you, your family, and Audrey will be taken to a secure location. It looks increasingly like Joint Base Lewis-McChord will be the choice."

"Have there been any other incidents?" asked Kim as she gently patted her daughter Guadalupe's back. Brenna was rocking and cooing at Kim's son Rex.

"Not yet. You and Audrey are the prime targets, as Samuel blames you two for uncovering their schemes. Plus, the death of his sister."

"Check with the Richards," interjected Audrey. "Their dogs did some personal damage to the Neilsens."

"No report from the protection agents assigned there, but we will call and double-check," replied Marcia Bernal. "Then, they and others may join you in lockdown."

Richard Johnson walked up to the small group as some Agents helped load a body on a stretcher. "We have one survivor from the ass—I mean the attackers. He is on that stretcher and will be transported under lock and key to Madigan Military Hospital."

"Who is he?" asked Kim.

"Local thug who has already admitted a Russian hired him. He wants a deal before he tells us more, as the guy said he will be dead if the Russians find out."

"So, no local Asian organized crime involved,"

said Kim.

"Not yet. But WEG has some long tentacles, it seems. Money talks, and we know he has millions hidden."

"I wonder why Samuel did not hire some former special operations types," said Audrey. "This group just did a full assault, no finesse, and not that efficient either. It looks like we have about seven dead miscreants and one prisoner."

"You know, this may be more about the pure creation of fear than trying to whack Audrey and me," interjected Kim. "Thus, they use expendable thugs rather than trained operatives. That is a lot cheaper at the end of the day."

"Could be," replied the FBI ASAC. "At the end of this day, yes, they scared the crap out of us supervisors. Time to ensure that does not happen again."

18.

Samuel Neilsen watched the breaking news at Midnight about the attack at Kim Kupar's home and laughed. It had the expected effect. The government would be rushing around to prevent further questions about their competency. After all, there had been a full-fledged assault in quiet suburbia because the government allowed material witnesses to live at home with minimal protection in a vast and vital case.

Samuel sat in a cheap mobile home in a Kitsap County trailer park. He knew the government would immediately decide that Samuel would travel as far away as possible from the locations of his alleged crimes. They were wrong. Hiding in plain sight was very easy if you made efforts to blend in. No flashy clothes, cars, expensive hotel rooms, and staying at some estate was not for him. He already had a Hollywood-style fake but natural-looking beard to change his features and would venture out only at night. He also avoided areas with surveillance cameras in case someone used facial recognition software.

When the main door to the mobile home opened, Samuel turned towards it with a Glock automatic in his hand.

"No worries, Samuel. I, Dima Volkov, am back with some decent food and drink."

Samuel laid the pistol on the small end table next to his recliner as the sizable black-bearded Russian entered the mobile home.

"Can't be too careful, Dima. Have you listened to the radio?"

"Yes, Samuel. The rather cheaply hired muscle performed as expected. They produced lots of noise and bullet holes, but the targets still walked around at last report."

"Well, comrade, they performed as I wished. They know little about who and why they were hired; the guns and vehicles used are not traceable to anyone connected to your organization or mine.

Dima smiled as he put away the food. "Have you heard from the location here in Kitsap?"

Samuel glanced at his cell phone clock as he answered. "They should be commencing their operation any time now," Samuel said as he looked up at Dima. "I hope to have two canine skins before the sun rises."

A large dark snout and a canine tongue woke up John Richards. He reached out to pet Blackie and the unique dog took John's hand in his mouth. Blackie gently pulled John to get up from the bed.

"What's up, big fella?" John whispered as he heard and felt Rebecca stir.

Blackie kept gently pulling on John's hand until he stood up.

"John?" a sleepy Rebecca asked.

"Go back to sleep, Babe. Blackie is just restless."

As John followed Blackie to the back door, Snow met them. "What are you two up to? You'll wake the kids." Both dogs looked at the backdoor in a way that John had learned meant something was out there they wanted to check out. At that time, his Combat Spidey Sense tingled.

John slipped on a pair of beat-up running shoes that Rebecca demanded he not use to walk on the carpet. He reached into the nearby closet and removed the flashlight-attached tactical shotgun. Quickly removing the combination trigger lock, he turned on the floodlights he'd installed after some late-night unwanted visitors. Knowing the high-beam lights aiming out into the surrounding yard would blind anyone sneaking up, he opened the door and let the two K-9s out. In a flash, they were gone. John quickly stepped out and off the porch, crouching behind some lawn furniture. The government's two-person security team was nowhere to be seen.

Now outside, John thought he heard some whispering from an extensive orchard that gave the residence Orchard House its name. John tried to see past the lights as a shriek emanated behind several apple trees. Based on John's experience, it sounded like canine teeth-filled jaws were abusing someone's genitals.

Muzzle flashes joined the reports of assault weapons and loud voices cursing in various languages. A figure with a gun came running in a panic toward the house. John let the individual feel a lot of buckshot as he yelled, "Stop right there, all of you!"

A bullet buzzed by his ear, and he flattened to the ground. He knew Rebecca would be up in a flash, armed to protect Jack and Jill and telephoning the police. John concentrated on target acquisition as it dawned on him that he was in a gunfight wearing nothing but skivvies. He picked out a two-legged silhouette parallel to the porch and took the legs out with a load of buckshot. Someone's scream was cut off in mid-voice, and then John heard someone yell, "*Run!*"

The twin wraiths of Blackie and Snow had sent the assailants retreating in a panic. John yelled, "Out," to return the dogs to the house. Blackie ran toward him, barked once, and took off in pursuit of retreating figures.

"*John!*" Rebecca screamed from the house.

"Call the cops and Kim and Audrey," he yelled back. "Tell them Neilsen struck."

He started running after the dogs. They were on the scent and were family. They would not give up until the threat to their pack was neutralized.

"Damned hardheaded dogs," John cursed as he ran. Not for the first time did he wonder who was in charge, humans or canines.

Kim was packing for a Joint Base Lewis McChord trip when her cell phone rang. She answered, "Agent Kupar."

"Rebecca Richards here. Neilsen tried to take us out. John and the dogs are in pursuit; damn their eyes."

"Protect your kids," said Kim. "The cavalry is on the way."

Samuel and Dima were having a late-night snack when someone began pounding at the mobile home's front door. Samuel grabbed his pistol and hid behind the couch as Dima picked up his Skorpion machine pistol and stepped to the door. The Russian peered through the peephole, then spoke in Russian. The person knocking replied in Russian, and Dima let a rather frazzled-looking, dark-haired, and bearded man in. After a short conversation with the sweaty and disheveled Russian, Dima opened the door again, and the man quickly left.

"Who was that?" asked Samuel.

"One of the transport drivers for the team

assigned to take out Richard's dogs."

"You told him to come here with me?"

Dima gave Samuel a cold stare.

"I am not stupid. He does not know you are staying here and has no idea who you are. I do not share with the foot soldiers who hired me and mine."

"Someone may have followed him here," Samuel snarled. "I picked this out-of-the-way place to be off the grid. I could be staying in the lap of luxury under an assumed name."

"But you didn't. You trusted me. I have done everything as you asked."

"So what happened at the Richards house?" demanded Samuel.

"The dogs were not killed. Two security agents were killed with crossbows. The house was alerted, and a firefight ensued."

Dima paused as he fixed Samuel with a cold dark stare. "Well, go on, Dima. What happened then?"

"Those not normal dogs and the former Pararescueman killed or wounded all but one hireling. He made it to Dasha's vehicle to tell him what happened."

"Damn! I thought you had good people working for you."

Dima paused again and walked over to a kitchen cupboard. He removed a bottle of Vodka and two glasses and then sat back at the dining table. Samuel finally took the hint and joined him as Dimi poured two glasses of Vodka.

"If you remember, Samuel, I told you to do this quickly, with little planning, with ignorant personnel, the chances of success were greatly reduced."

Dima drank the Vodka in one gulp and then poured himself another. "The personnel who rescued you from detention were all former Russian Special Forces."

"I know that," snapped Samuel.

Dima gave the person known as Baby Bear another cold stare. Then he spoke again. "I arranged forty-eight hours of training on snatching you from the Americans."

"I realize—"

Dima held up a hand to stop the comment. "I then had them disappear for their safety and yours. If no one involved can be questioned, no one will know where you may have gone."

"So what does—"

Another palm up to stop the statement. "You are fixated with a vengeance, now. You lack the patience to allow for a well-planned operation. I have learned in many years of such activities that revenge is a dish best-served cold. It allows you to savor the expectation and provides the necessary time for adequate planning." Dima threw the Vodga down the back of his throat. He looked at Samuel. "Your Vodka is going to waste."

"I am not much of a drinker," replied Samuel.

"You should try it. Drinking can calm you down and relax you when done right."

"I have more important concerns. Such as ensuring the tasks I paid you handsomely for are completed satisfactorily."

Dima smiled at the kidnapper of children as he poured himself another shot. "I understand the one known as Baby Rabbit was a medical doctor."

"Yes. She helped keep the children calm and healthy."

"My sources also say her skills were used in interrogating the women and children of certain claimed enemies of the United States."

"Yes, but what does—"

"Yet you claim your mission was about protecting little children from abuse. Don't you think the techniques she used to obtain information would classify as abuse?"

Samuel's brow furrowed in confusion and concentration. "What has that to do with anything? Are you suddenly developing a conscience about the tasks I paid you for over the last week?"

Dimi laughed. "Oh, no," the large Russian replied. "I have done the same. Pain applied to one's family clarifies the understanding of the situation."

"Then why the questions, Dima?"

"Because my supposed comrade, I found out today that the one known as Baby Rabbit was, shall we say, involved in the questioning of the families of some of my associates."

"I, I, I, did not know that," stuttered Samuel.

"You should have," Dima said as he fired a three-round burst from the Skorpion into the face of Baby Bear. Samuel toppled off of his chair and onto the floor.

Dima stood and admired his work for a moment, then spoke. "I consistently fulfill the paid contract. I did that tonight. I never cheat my employer." The Russian spat on the body. "You should always know the baggage your employees bring. Sometimes a suitcase can explode." Dima gulped down the untouched shot of Vodka. "You are also not the only one who seeks vengeance on those who harm one's family. I will deal with the one named Baby Rabbit."

John Richards was glad he kept in shape as he figured he had run some five miles in the dark. One of the dogs would fall back and check to see if he was still following them as they loped along. John remembered reading somewhere that humans were the one species that could match or beat canines in a long-distance run. John wondered if they meant early hominids, not today's humanity.

He had seen a dark-clothed figure jump into a blacked-out SUV at the end of Orchard House's long driveway. He knew the dogs could follow the scent of a vehicle if given the time for a good scent picture. They may not be able to follow a car for miles and miles, but locally they have a good chance. Blackie and Snow were remarkable canines, so if any dogs could, they were the ones.

Snow appeared at the entranceway to a dirt driveway off an Olalla area paved road. She saw John running some fifty yards away and gave a low "gruff" to draw his attention. Once she had it, she turned and trotted down the road. John swore under his breath and tried to pick up the pace.

The small dirt road led past aged trailers to a mobile home that had seen better days. Lights on the inside proved it was still occupied as someone was paying the electric bill. Snow and Blackie disappeared into the surrounding darkness as John stealthily approached. The Pararescue NCO was always good at sneakypete on active duty and believed he kept that ability in retirement. As he closed within twenty-five yards of the home, the front door opened, and the interior lights silhouetted a prominent figure.

John crouched in the shadows as he watched the person walk to a black SUV and remove a gas can lashed to the roof. The man seemed to be singing some song in Russian as he set about spreading gasoline around the base of the mobile home. John knew anyone about to light a fire in a mobile home in the middle of the night must be up to no good. As John snuck closer, a black shape exploded from the dark.

Blackie slammed into the Russian with such force

that an imprint of the large man was pushed into the mobile home siding. The gas can was knocked away, and the man collapsed, stunned. John stood over the man within seconds, realizing he had no cell phone to call the police. Snow joined her mate, and John entered the residence to find a phone. "Watch him," John commanded the dogs, despite the fact they were already performing that function. John called out, "Hello, Doordash," as he entered with his shotgun at the ready.

He saw the Skorpion machine pistol on the dinner table beside a bottle of Vodka. As he stepped closer, he saw the body lying in a pool of blood. The bullets mutilated the face so that identification would be a problem. An old-style wall phone was mounted near the front door. John picked it up and received an excellent old-fashioned dial tone. He punched in numbers, and someone answered, "9-1-1; Is this an emergency?"

"I am in a mobile home with a dead body, which qualifies as an emergency. Let me see if I can find something with an address on it."

Three hours later, Kim Kupar walked up to a hot coffee-drinking John Richards in a lawn chair outside the mobile home.

"You should be home with your children," said the Special Agent with a smile.

"I could say the same to you, Agent Kupar." With a grin, John added, "Or is it, Tiger Lady?"

"I will never live that down it seems."

"Hell, Lady. You chased a mutated tiger around Kitsap County. Things like that are not forgotten."

"Neither will the Night Time Run of the Pararescueman and his K-9 friends be forgotten. You and your furry family helped wrap up the Neilsen escape investigation."

John shrugged and sipped his coffee. "If they hadn't attacked my home, I would still be there. Neilsen really wanted revenge on the dogs, didn't he?"

"It seems. Undoubtedly, the Russians you and your dogs took down have information about tonight's events here and at my home."

"Think they will talk?"

Now it was Kim's turn to shrug as she replied, "Who knows? But I bet forensics will show this one shot is Samuel, AKA Baby Bear. As much as that killing simplifies the investigation, this Dima Volkov will still have to answer for Samuel's death. Not to mention his involvement in the death of two LEOs at your home."

"Yep. That should not have happened. We also still have the other minions to prosecute."

"Most are looking for plea deals, John. Once they heard about the history of Kelly Parsons and the secret plans of the Neilsens for escape, they started singing like canaries."

"They will claim they were used and kept in the dark, Kim."

"But they knew the children were not voluntarily at the various installations. They will all have to face kidnapping charges."

Audrey DiStefano approached the pair with two fresh cups of coffee and one tea.

"Marines bearing gifts, I see," said John with a grin.

"We have to take care of the Chair Force, Chief," replied the FBI Agent,

"Which is fine by me," replied John as he grinned and took the offered coffee.

"You ready to write a statement?" asked Audrey.

"Already did. Used the Kitsap Sheriff's statement forms as they arrived first."

"Well, my agency will want more statements on their forms. Lead agency and all that protocol crap."

"Can I get some rest first?"

"Of course. We'll give you a ride home with your beasties."

Snow and Blackie sat in the shadows watching the Two Legs making noises they knew were a form of communication. John felt their eyes on him and looked at the two extraordinary dogs. "Those dogs ran my ass off. I have blisters from my running shoes with no socks."

"Glad someone found you some sweatpants, Chief. Parading around in tidy whities will shock the sensibilities of some of the female personnel."

"But not you, I suspect."

"Former Marine, remember? I have seen lots of male testicles hanging out."

"And kicked some of them, right?"

"You got that right."

As the three humans chuckled, Snow and Blackie looked at each other. Silent communication expressed the notion that they would never fully understand Two Legs. However, there would always be love for them.

19.

After the awards ceremony, there was an obligatory reception with cheap punch and light snacks. Of course, some cop spiked one of the punch bowls with Vodka, so many there soon had a buzz on. Kim and Hank had Kim's mother looking after and spoiling their twins. Sitting to one side were John, Rebecca, their twins, and the two dogs. Snow and Blackie were soaking up all the added attention from the former kidnapped children, led by Grette.

"This one here, Snow, saved me," the young girl said with the utmost sincerity. Grette hugged Snow as she told the other children, "If she has puppies, Mommie says we can have one."

"You two are lucky these beasties picked you," John told Jack and Jill.

"We know, Dad," said Jack. "They saved us."

"Your dad helped also," said Rebecca.

"We know," said Jill, who then hugged her father.

"The medals look good on you and the dogs," added Rebecca.

"So does yours, Babe. Just remember you started all this."

"Actually, Snow did. But who am I to disagree?" With that, she kissed her husband.

Audrey walked up to Kim and Hank with two glasses of punch.

"Nice pants suit," said Hank.

"Boss tried to get me to wear a dress," said Audrey. "I told her Kim would wear one representing both of us."

"Forever the stubborn Marine, I see," said Kim with a grin.

"Hey, I am too set in my ways to change now."

"Did you and Kathy Mueller come as a—couple?"

"Nosey, aren't we?"

"Remember when we started this investigation, Audrey? You said you were jealous that I found a mate for life, and I said—"

"I know. You and Hank would help me find Miss Right."

"So I guess that assistance is no longer required."

Audrey looked at the red-headed AUSA. "So far,

it's been—great. We've had to work closely to get this prosecution put to bed. One thing led to another and, well—"

Kim reached over and squeezed her investigative partner's arm. "So one good thing came out of this strange case. Other than recovering all the missing children alive and without serious harm."

"And the Neilsens had Karma bite them in the ass—especially Samuel, with the Russian shooting him in the face just when he thought he had things under control."

"Samuel's psychosis got the best of him. He thought he was above reproach."

"He is dead now," interjected Hank. "It looks like Kim will have a break from risking obtaining more scars and injuries by being an instructor. Like you, Audrey, she is being promoted to Senior Special Agent."

The FBI Agent blushed a bit at the mention of the promotion. "Yeah. I just did my job. Without Tiger Lady here, I'd probably ride a desk instead of being sent to Quantico."

"Without you, Audrey, I might not be here in one piece."

The two women looked into each other's eyes and smiled. Then they embraced. "We make great Pardners, as T-rex would say," Kim said as she held back tears. "I'm going to miss you."

"Hey, Quantico is not that far from FLETC. We can

visit, and I can spoil the twins."

The two special agents stepped back from the embrace and held hands. "I'll treat you to a night at *PAMS NUMBER #1* in Brunswick, Georgia. It is claimed to be the largest law enforcement bar around."

"I'll hold you to that, Kim Kupar. A fun old drinking night on the town will do this Former Marine some good."

At that moment, a young manchild in a suit walked up to them. Bahadur Jaswal had already thanked Snow, Blackie, and the Richards for helping rescue his sister Grette. Now he approached Kim and Audrey with unique gifts.

"I have something for you," the young boy said, "I made them myself."

He handed a rolled-up and tied it with a large ribbon paper to each. The two agents grinned and accepted them. "Why, thank you, young man," said Audrey. "What have we—" They were matching sharp intakes of breath from the two women.

Audrey held an intricate drawing of her in a Marine Corps Uniform, descending from the sky in full combat regalia. Kim's unrolled picture was her as the Hindu Goddess Durga atop a giant tiger.

"*The Great Rescue*" was written in large gold letters on each artwork.

"You saved my sister, Grette," said, Bahadur. "And all of her new friends. That needs to be recorded forever and ever."

Kim bent over and hugged the boy to her. "This is better than any medal," she said.

Audrey reached over and added a hug. "I will frame this and mount it in a place of honor," said Audrey as her eyes filled with tears. "This is better than any commendation or award."

Bahadur grinned at the two special agents and said. "I am glad you like it. Now I must go back to my parents. They still want us to stay close. See you later."

The young man turned and proudly walked back to his parents, the mission complete.

"This is better than just about anything I have received," said Audrey.

"I know, Audrey. That is because it is from genuine heartfelt appreciation. Not some attempt at a ceremony."

Hank stepped up and hugged both women. "Just remember how special you are and what you did. Without you two, this good would not have happened."

"Uffda," said Audrey as he tried to escape Hank's grasp. "Does he always squeeze you this hard?"

"Welcome to my world of living with the modern Hercules," said Kim. "It has its moments."

The three laughed and then went for refills of punch. It was a good day, one of many to come for them, their friend, and their families.

Dima Volkov sat patiently in the Federal Detention Center. Before he embraced a profitable crime career, his time in Russian Intelligence had taught him how to wait. His former employment with the Russian government would now pay off, especially as he had bribed many an official with the profits he had accrued.

After he gave information on the non-Russian minions of WEG and the Neilsens (he owed no loyalty), someone in the Russian government contacted the U.S. about a swap of prisoners. Dima managed to convince the investigators that his role was minor. It helped when he told them why he had killed Samuel. He knew of the operations and activities Kelly Parsons performed in the past for U.S.-sanctioned intelligence programs. If Dima or Baby Rabbit went to trial, the details of those actions would hit the public like a bomb. Abu Ghraib, for children, would destroy careers and send some influential people to prison. Not to mention that some past criminal cases might be in danger. The United States was already weakened worldwide with images of people falling off military transport aircraft and bodies in the Rio Grande. Anything similar which could be avoidable would be dodged.

Dima Volkov also calmly waited as he knew he

would soon hear about some arrangements he was working on concerning Kelly Parsons. He had not forgotten what she had done to some Russian families.

Revenge was a dish best-served cold. Samuel Neilsen was too unbalanced to understand that concept. His psychotic passion had killed him and his sister and destroyed the so-called mission. Dimi laid back on the prison bunk and sighed.

American prisons were like hotels compared to Russian camps. In moments, Dima was in dreamless sleep. He was far from innocent, but he slept well.

At the daycare and playground near the U.S. Federal Building on Second Avenue in Seattle, Washington, Ebony and Red welcomed two new children to the group.

"So, Wendy," said Ebony, "Jimmy Brown here says you're a mean one with a sharpened pencil."

"She kept me from being kidnapped," interjected Jimmy. "Then I helped the two Agents who caught the bad people."

Red smiled at the now two best friends.

"You're a brave young lady, Wendy," said Red. "Promise me you'll only stab people trying to run off with any of the other children."

Wendy gave Red a quizzical look. "Why would I stab anyone else?"

The two adults suppressed laughter as they did not want young Wendy to feel put upon by two unfamiliar adults. Since the culmination of the Rainbow Investigation, Red and Ebony were hired on as staff for the daycare and playground. The Jaswals had led a formal movement for funds to support such an effort. Kim Kupar's father had ensured the funds were made available by donations from his and other local businesses.

"No child should fear abduction in our society," Balraj Singh Kupar said in a news conference. The fact that his daughter Kim was one of the heroes in rescuing the thirteen kidnapped children added extra weight to the money the businessman donated to the cause. Other businesses followed suit. And thus, Red and Ebony were certified and paid childcare professionals, something they would gladly do for free as their children were involved.

Wendy took charge of her best friend, Jimmy, and led him to the monkey bars.

"Well. All's well that ends well," said Ebony.

"Getting philosophical?" asked Red.

"It's just had to believe everything started when a four-year-old was grabbed. And then everything came together just right, so all the kids made it home safely."

"Well, we'll make sure that never happens again, won't we?"

"Hell, yeah, Partner," replied Ebony. "After all, we

have a dangerous secret weapon."

"What's that, Pard?"

"A young white girl with a sharp number two pencil."

All the children turned to watch the two crazy adult women laugh until they cried.

9 781590 928950